# TRUE TO HIMSELF

## ROGER STRONG'S STRUGGLE FOR PLACE

## EDWARD STRATEMEYER

1st WORLD
LIBRARY
Literary Society

# True to Himself

## Edward Stratemeyer

© 1st World Library, 2007
PO Box 2211
Fairfield, IA 52556
www.1stworldlibrary.com
First Edition

LCCN: 2007901779

Softcover ISBN: 978-1-4218-4247-9
Hardcover ISBN: 978-1-4218-4149-6
eBook ISBN: 978-1-4218-4345-2

Purchase *"True to Himself"*
as a traditional bound book at:
www.1stWorldLibrary.com/purchase.asp?ISBN=978-1-4218-4247-9

1st World Library is a literary, educational organization
dedicated to:

- Creating a free internet library of downloadable ebooks

- Hosting writing competitions and offering book publishing
scholarships.

Interested in more 1st World Library books? contact:
literacy@1stworldlibrary.com
Check us out at: www.1stworldlibrary.com

# 1ˢᵗ World Library Literary Society

## Giving Back to the World

"If you want to work on the core problem, it's early school literacy."

**- James Barksdale, former CEO of Netscape**

"No skill is more crucial to the future of a child, or to a democratic and prosperous society, than literacy."

**- Los Angeles Times**

Literacy... means far more than learning how to read and write... The aim is to transmit... knowledge and promote social participation."

**- UNESCO**

"Literacy is not a luxury, it is a right and a responsibility. If our world is to meet the challenges of the twenty-first century we must harness the energy and creativity of all our citizens."

**- President Bill Clinton**

"Parents should be encouraged to read to their children, and teachers should be equipped with all available techniques for teaching literacy, so the varying needs and capacities of individual kids can be taken into account."

**- Hugh Mackay**

# PREFACE

"True to himself," while a complete story in itself, forms the third volume of the "Ship and Shore Series," tales of adventure on land and sea, written for both boys and girls.

In this story we are introduced to Roger Strong, a typical American country lad, and his sister Kate, who, by an unhappy combination of events, are thrown upon their own resources and compelled to make their own way in the world.

To make one's way in the world is, ordinarily, difficult enough; but when one is handicapped by a cloud on the family name, the difficulty becomes far greater. With his father thrown into prison on a serious charge, Roger finds that few people will have anything to do with either himself or his sister, and the jeers flung at him are at times almost more than he can bear. But he is "true to himself" in the best meaning of that saying, rising above those who would pull him down, and, in the end, not only succeeds in making a place for himself in the world, but also scores a worthy triumph over those who had caused his parents' downfall.

When this story was first printed as a serial, the author has every reason to believe it was well received by the boys and girls for whom it was written. In its present revised form he hopes it will meet with equal commendation.

Edward Stratemeyer. Newark, N.J., April 15, 1900.

# CHAPTER I

## THE TROUBLE IN THE ORCHARD

"Hi, there, Duncan Woodward!" I called out. "What are you doing in Widow Canby's orchard?"

"None of your business, Roger Strong," replied the only son of the wealthiest merchant in Darbyville.

"You are stealing her pears," I went on. "Your pockets are full of them."

"See here, Roger Strong, just you mind your own business and leave me alone."

"I am minding my business," I rejoined warmly.

"Indeed!" And Duncan put as much of a sneer as was possible in the word.

"Yes, indeed. Widow Canby pays me for taking care of her orchard, and that includes keeping an eye on these pear trees," and I approached the tree upon the lowest branch of which Duncan was standing.

"Humph! You think you're mighty big!" he blustered, as he

jumped to the ground. "What right has a fellow like you to talk to me in this manner? You are getting too big for your boots."

"I don't think so. I'm guarding this property, and I want you to hand over what you've taken and leave the premises," I retorted, for I did not fancy the style in which I was being addressed.

"Pooh! Do you expect me to pay any attention to that?"

"You had better, Duncan. If you don't you may get into trouble."

"I suppose you intend to tell the widow what I've done."

"I certainly shall; unless you do as I've told you to."

Duncan bit his lip. "How do you know but what the widow said I could have the pears?" he ventured.

"If she did, it's all right," I returned, astonished, not so much over the fact that Widow Canby had granted the permission, as that such a high-toned young gentleman as Duncan Woodward should desire that privilege.

"You've no business to jump at conclusions," he added sharply.

"If I judged you wrongly, I beg your pardon, Duncan. I'll speak to the widow about it."

I began to move off toward the house. Duncan hurried after me and caught me by the arm.

"You fool you, what do you mean?" he demanded.

"I'm going to find out if you are telling the truth."

"Isn't my word enough?"

"It will do no harm to ask," I replied evasively, not caring to pick a quarrel, and yet morally sure that he was prevaricating.

"So you think I'm telling you a falsehood? I've a good mind to give you a sound drubbing," he cried angrily.

Duncan Woodward had many of the traits of a bully about him. He was the only son of a widower who nearly idolized him, and, lacking a mother's guiding influence, he had grown up wayward in the extreme.

He was a tall, well-built fellow, strong from constant athletic exercise, and given, on this account, to having his way among his associates.

Yet I was not afraid of him. Indeed, to tell the truth, I was not afraid of any one. For eight years I had been shoved in life from pillar to post, until now threats had no terrors for me.

Both of my parents were dead to me. My mother died when I was but five years old. She was of a delicate nature, and, strange as it may seem, I am inclined to believe that it was for the best that her death occurred when it did. The reason I believe this is, because she was thus spared the disgrace that came upon our family several years later.

At her death my father was employed as head clerk by the firm of Holland & Mack, wholesale provision merchants of Newville, a thriving city which was but a few miles from Darbyville, a pretty village located on the Pass River.

We occupied a handsome house in the centre of the village. Our family, besides my parents and myself, contained but one other member— my sister Kate, who was several years my senior.

When our beloved mother died, Kate took the management of our home upon her shoulders, and as she had learned, during my mother's long illness, how everything should be done, our domestic affairs ran smoothly. All this time I attended the Darbyville school, and was laying the foundation for a commercial education, intending at some later day to follow in the footsteps of my father.

Two years passed, and then my father's manner changed. From being bright and cheerful toward us he became moody and silent. What the cause was I could not guess, and it did not help matters to be told by Duncan Woodward, whose father was also employed by Holland & Mack, that "some folks would soon learn what was what, and no mistake."

At length the thunderbolt fell. Returning from school one day, I found Kate in tears.

"Oh, Roger!" she burst out. "They say father has stolen money from Holland & Mack, and they have just arrested him for a thief!"

The blow was a terrible one. I was but a boy of fourteen, and the news completely bewildered me. I put on my cap, and together with Kate, took the first horse car to Newville to find out what it all meant.

We found my father in jail, where he had been placed to await the action of the grand jury. It was with difficulty that we obtained permission to see him, and ascertained the facts of the case.

Edward Stratemeyer

The charge against him was for raising money upon forged cheeks, eight in number, the total amount being nearly twelve thousand dollars. The name of the firm had been forged, and the money collected in New York and Brooklyn. I was not old enough to understand the particulars.

My father protested his innocence, but it was of no avail. The forgery was declared to be his work, and, though it was said that he must have had an accomplice to obtain the money, he was adjudged the guilty party.

"Ten years in the State's prison." That was the penalty. My father grew deadly white, while as for me, my very heart seemed to stop beating. Kate fainted, and two days later the doctor announced that she had an attack of brain fever.

Two months dragged slowly by. Then my sister was declared to be out of danger. Next the house was sold over our heads, and we were turned out upon the world, branded as the children of a thief, to get a living as best we could.

Both of us would willingly have left Darbyville, but where should we go? The only relation we had was an uncle,— Captain Enos Moss,—and he was on an extended trip to South America, and when he would return no one knew.

All the friends we had had before deserted us. The girls "turned up their noses" at Kate,—which made my blood boil,—and the boys fought shy of me.

I tried to find work, but without success. Even in places where help was wanted excuses were made to me—trivial excuses that meant but one thing—that they did not desire any one in their employ who had a stain upon his name.

Kate was equally unsuccessful; and we might have starved

but for a lucky incident that happened just as we were ready to give up in despair.

Walking along the road one day, I saw Farmer Tilford's bull tearing across the field toward a gate which had been accidentally left open. The Widow Canby, absorbed in thought and quite unconscious of the danger that threatened her, was just passing this gate, when I darted forward and closed it just a second before the bull reached it. I did not consider my act an heroic one, but the Widow Canby declared it otherwise.

"You are a brave boy," she said. "Who are you?"

I told her, coloring as I spoke. But she laid a kindly hand upon my shoulder.

"Even if your father was guilty, you are not to blame," she said, and she made me tell her all about myself, and about Kate, and the hard luck we were having.

The Widow Canby lived in an old-fashioned house, surrounded on three sides by orchards several acres in extent. She was well to do, but made no pretence to style. Many thought her extremely eccentric but that was only because they did not know her.

The day I came to her assistance she made me stay to supper, and when I left it was under promise to call the next day and bring my sister along.

This I did, and a long conversation took place, which resulted in Kate and myself going to live with the widow—I to take care of the garden and the orchards, and my sister to help with the housekeeping, for which we received our board and joint wages of fifteen dollars per month.

Edward Stratemeyer

We could not have fallen into better hands. Mrs. Canby was as considerate as one would wish, and had it not been for the cloud upon our name we would have been content.

But the stain upon our family was a source of unpleasantness to us. I fully believed my father innocent, and I wondered if the time would ever come when his character would be cleared.

My duties around Widow Canby's place were not onerous, and I had plenty of chance for self-improvement. I had finished my course at the village school in spite of the calumny that was cast upon me, and now I continued my studies in private whenever the opportunity offered.

I was looked down upon by nearly every one in the village. To strangers I was pointed out as the convict's son, and people reckoned that the "Widder Canby wasn't right sharp when she took in them as wasn't to be trusted."

I was not over-sensitive, but these remarks, which generally reached my ears sooner or later, made me very angry. What right had people to look down on my sister and myself? It was not fair to Kate and me, and I proposed to stand it no longer.

It was a lovely morning in September, but I was in no mood to enjoy the bright sunshine and clear air that flooded the orchard. I had just come from the depot with the mail for Mrs. Canby, and down there I had heard two men pass opinions on my father's case that were not only uncharitable but unjust.

I was therefore in no frame of mind to put up with Duncan Woodward's actions, and when he spoke of giving me a good drubbing I prepared to defend myself.

"Two can play at that game, Duncan," I replied.

"Ho! ho! Do you mean to say you can stand up against me?" he asked derisively.

"I can try," I returned stoutly. "I'm sure now that you have no business here."

"Why, you miserable little thief—"

"Stop that! I'm no thief, if you please."

"Well, you're the son of one, and that's the same thing."

"My father is innocent, and I won't allow any one, big or little, to call him a thief," I burst out. "Some day he will be cleared."

"Not much!" laughed Duncan. "My father knows all about the case. I can tell you that."

"Then perhaps he knows where the money went to," I replied quickly. "I know he was very intimate with my father at that time."

Had I stopped to think I would not have spoken as I did. My remark made the young man furious, and I had hardly spoken before Duncan hit me a stinging blow on the forehead, and, springing upon me, bore me to the ground.

Edward Stratemeyer

# CHAPTER II

## AN ASSAULT ON THE ROAD

I knew Duncan Woodward would not hesitate to attack me. He was a much larger fellow than myself, and always ready to fight any one he thought he could whip.

Yet I was not prepared for the sudden onslaught that had been made. Had I been, I might have parried his blow.

But I did not intend to be subdued as easily as he imagined. The blow on my forehead pained not a little, and it made me mad "clear through."

"Get off of me!" I cried, as Duncan brought his full weight down upon my chest.

"Not much! Not until you promise to keep quiet about this affair," he replied.

"If you don't get off, you'll be mighty sorry;" was my reply, as I squirmed around in an effort to throw him aside.

Suddenly he caught me by the ear, and gave that member a twist that caused me to cry out with pain.

"Now will you do as I say?" he demanded.

"No"

Again he caught my ear. But now I was ready for him. It was useless to try to shake him off. He was too heavy and powerful for that. So I brought a small, but effective weapon into play. The weapon was nothing more than a pin that held together a rent in my trousers made the day previous. Without hesitation I pulled it out and ran it a good half-inch into his leg.

The yell be gave would have done credit to a wild Indian, and he bounded a distance of several feet. I was not slow to take advantage of this movement, and in an instant I was on my feet and several yards away.

Duncan's rage knew no bounds. He was mad enough to "chew me up," and with a loud exclamation he sprang after me, aiming a blow at my head as he did so.

I dodged his arm, and then, gathering myself together, landed my fist fairly and squarely upon the tip of his nose, a blow that knocked him off his feet and sent him rolling to the ground.

To say that I was astonished at what I had done would not express my entire feelings. I was amazed, and could hardly credit my own eyesight. Yet there he lay, the blood flowing from the end of his nasal organ. He was completely knocked out, and I had done the deed. I did not fear for consequences. I felt justified in what I had done. But I wondered how Duncan would stand the punishment.

With a look of intense bitterness on his face he rose slowly to his feet. The blood was running down his chin, and there were several stains upon his white collar and his shirt front. If a look could have crushed me I would have been instantly annihilated.

"I'll fix you for that!" he roared. "Roger Strong, I'll get even with you, if it takes ten years!"

"Do what you please, Duncan Woodward," I rejoined. "I don't fear you. Only beware how you address me in the future. You will get yourself into trouble."

"I imagine you will be the one to get into trouble," he returned insinuatingly.

"I'm not afraid. But—hold up there!" I added, for Duncan had begun to move off toward the fence.

"What for?"

"I want you to hand over the pears you picked."

"I won't."

"Very well. Then I'll report the case to Mrs. Canby."

Duncan grew white.

"Take your confounded fruit," he howled, throwing a dozen or more of the luscious pears at my feet. "If I don't get even with you, my name isn't Duncan Woodward!"

And with this parting threat he turned to the fence, jumped over, and strode down the road.

In spite of the seriousness of the affair I could not help but laugh. Duncan had no doubt thought it a great lark to rob the widow's orchard, never dreaming of the wrong he was doing or of the injury to the trees. Now his nose was swollen, his clothes soiled, and he had suffered defeat in every way.

I had no doubt that he would do all in his power to get even with me. He hated me and always had. At school I had surpassed him in our studies, and on the ball field I had proved myself a superior player. I do not wish to brag about what I did, but it is necessary to show why Duncan disliked me.

Nor was there much love lost on my side, though I always treated him fairly. The reason for this was plain.

As I have stated, his father, Aaron Woodward, was at one tune a fellow-clerk with my father. At the time my father was arrested, Woodward was one of his principal accusers. Duncan had, of course, taken up the matter. Since then Mr. Woodward had received a large legacy from a dead relative in Chicago, or its suburbs, and started the finest general store in Darbyville. But his bitterness toward us still continued.

That the man knew something about the money that had been stolen I did not doubt, but how to prove it was a difficult problem that I had pondered many times without arriving at any satisfactory conclusion.

I watched Duncan out of sight and then turned and walked slowly toward the house.

"Roger!"

It was Mrs. Canby who called me. She stood on the side porch with a letter in her hand.

"You want me?"

"Yes, I have quite important news," she continued. "My sister in Norfolk is very ill, and I must go to her at once. I have spoken to Kate about it. Do you think you can get along while I am gone?"

"Yes, ma'am. How long do you expect to be away?"

"If she is not seriously ill I shall be back by day after to-morrow. You can hitch up Jerry at once. The train leaves in an hour."

"I'll have him at the door in five minutes."

"And, Roger, you and Kate must take good care of things while I am gone. There are several hundred dollars locked up in my desk. I would take the money to the bank in Newville, only I hate to lose the time."

"I reckon it will be safe," I replied; "I'll keep good watch against burglars."

"Do you think you can handle a pistol?" she went on.

"I think I could," I replied, with all the interest of the average American boy in firearms.

"There is a pistol upstairs in my bureau that belonged to Mr. Canby. I will let you have that, though of course I trust you won't need it."

"Is it loaded?"

"Yes; I loaded it last week. I will lay it out before I go. Be very careful with it."

"I will," I promised her.

I hurried down to the barn, and in a few moments had Jerry hooked up to the family turnout. As I was about to jump in and drive to the house, a man confronted me.

He was a stranger, about forty years of age, with black hair and shaggy beard and eyebrows. He was seedily dressed, and altogether looked to be a disreputable character.

"Say, young man, can you help a fellow as is down on his luck?" he asked in a hoarse tone.

"Who are you?" I responded.

"I'm a moulder from Factoryville. The shop's shut down, and I'm out of money and out of work."

"How long have you been out?"

"Two weeks."

"And you haven't found work anywhere?"

"Not a stroke."

"Been to Newville?"

"All through it, and everything full."

I thought this was queer. I had glanced at the Want column of a Newville newspaper and had noted that moulders were wanted in several places.

The man's appearance did not strike me favorably, and when he came closer to me I noted that his breath smelt strongly of liquor.

Edward Stratemeyer

"I don't think I can help you," said I. "I have nothing for you to do."

"Give me a quarter, then, will you? I ain't had nothing to eat since yesterday."

"But you've had something to drink," I could not help remark.

The man scowled, "How do you know?"

"I can smell it on you."

"I only had one glass,—just to knock out a cold I caught. Come, make it half a dollar. I'll pay you back when I get work."

"I don't care to lend."

"Make it ten cents."

"Not a cent."

"You're mighty independent about it," he sneered.

"I have to be when such fellows as you tackle me," I returned with spirit.

"You're mighty high toned for a boy of your age."

"I'm too high toned to let you talk to me in this fashion. I want you to leave at once."

The tramp—for the man was nothing else—scowled worse than before.

"I'll leave when I please," he returned coolly.

I was nonplussed. I was in a hurry to get away to drive Widow Canby to the station. To leave the man hanging about the house with no one but my sister Kate home was simply out of the question.

Suddenly an idea struck me. Like most people who live in the country, Mrs. Canby kept a watch-dog—a large and powerful mastiff called Major. He was tied up near the back stoop out of sight, but could be pressed into service on short notice.

"If you don't go at once, I'll set the dog on you."

"Huh! You can't fool me!"

"No fooling about it. Major! Major!" I called.

There was a rattling of chain as the animal tried to break away, and then a loud barking. The noise seemed to strike terror to the tramp's heart.

"I'll get even with you, young fellow!" he growled, and running to the fence he scrambled over and out of sight. I did not wait to see in what direction he went.

When I reached the porch I found Mrs. Canby bidding my sister good-by. A moment more and she was on the seat. I touched up Jerry and we were off.

"It took you a long time to hitch up," the widow remarked as we drove along.

"It wasn't that," I replied, and told her about the tramp.

"You must be very careful of those men," she said anxiously. "Some of them will not stop at anything."

"I'll be wide awake," I rejoined reassuringly.

It was not a long drive to the station. When we arrived there, Mrs. Canby had over five minutes to spare, and this time was spent in buying a ticket and giving me final instructions.

At length the train came along and she was off. I waited a few moments longer and then drove away.

I had several purchases to make in the village—a pruning-knife, a bag of feed, and some groceries, and these took some time to buy, so it was nearly noon when I started home.

Several times I imagined that a couple of the village young men noticed me very closely, but I paid no attention and went on my way, never dreaming of what was in store for me.

The road to the widow's house ran for half a mile or more through a heavy belt of timber land. We were jogging along at a fair pace, and I was looking over a newspaper I had picked up on the station platform. Suddenly some one sprang out from the bushes and seized Jerry by the bridle.

Astonished and alarmed, I sprang up to see what was the matter. As I did so I received a stinging blow on the side of the head, and the next instant was dragged rudely from the carriage.

# CHAPTER III

## THE MODELS

I had been taken completely off my guard, but by instinct I tried to ward off my assailants. My effort was a useless one. In a trice I found myself on the ground, surrounded by half a dozen of the fastest young men to be found in Darbyville.

Prominent among them was Duncan Woodward, and I rightfully guessed that it was he who had organized the attack.

"Take it easy, Strong," exclaimed a fellow named Moran, "unless you want to be all broke up."

"What do you mean by treating me in this way?" I cried indignantly.

"You'll find out soon enough," said Phillips, another of the young men. "Come, stop your struggling."

"I'll do nothing of the kind. You have no right to molest me."

"Pooh!" sniffed Duncan. "The Models have a right to do anything."

"The Models?" I queried, in perplexity. "Who are they?"

Edward Stratemeyer

"The Models are a band of young gentlemen organized for the purpose of social enjoyment and to teach cads lessons that they are not likely to forget," replied Moran.

"I suppose you are the members," I said, surveying the half-dozen.

"We have that honor," rejoined a boy named Barton, who had not yet spoken.

"And we intend to teach you a lesson," added Pultzer, a short, stout chap, whose father had once been a butcher.

"What for?"

"For your unwarranted attack upon our illustrious president."

"Your president? You mean Duncan?"

"Mr. Woodward, if you please," interrupted Duncan, loftily. "I won't have such a low-bred fellow as you calling me by my first name."

"I'm no lower bred than you are," I retorted.

"Come, none of that!"cried Moran. "We all know you well. We shall at once proceed to teach you a lesson."

I could not help smile—the whole affair seemed so ridiculous that had it not been for the rough handling I had received when pulled from the carriage, I would have considered it a joke.

"You'll find it no laughing matter," said Duncan, savagely, angry, no doubt, because I did not show more signs of fear. "Just wait till we are through with you. You'll grin on the other side of your face."

"What do you intend to do with me?"

"You'll see soon enough."

I began to think the affair might be more serious than I had imagined. Six to one was heavy odds, and who could tell what these wild fellows would not do?

"I want you to let me go at once," I said decidedly. "If you don't, it will be the worse for you."

"Not a bit of it. We intend that you shall remember this occasion as long as you live," returned Moran. "Come, march along with us."

"Where to?"

"Never mind. March!"

For reply I turned, and made a hasty jump for the carriage, intending to utilize Jerry in a bold dash for liberty. I had just placed my foot upon the step and called to the horse when Moran caught me by the jacket and dragged me to the ground.

"No you don't!" he ejaculated roughly.

"There, Dunc, catch hold of him; and you too, Ellery. We mustn't let him escape after we've watched two hours to catch him!"

In an instant, I was surrounded. Now that Duncan had his friends to back him he was brave enough and held my arm in a grip of iron.

　　　　Edward Stratemeyer

"Any one bring a rope?" went on Moran.

"Here's one," replied Ellery Blake.

"Hand it over. We had better bind his hands."

Knowing that it would be folly to resist, I allowed them to do as Moran had advised. My wrists were knotted together behind my back, and then the cord was drawn tightly about my waist.

"Now march!"

"How about the horse and carriage?"

"They'll be O. K."

There seemed to be no help for it, so I walked along with them. Had there been the slightest chance offered to escape I would have taken it, but warned by experience, all six kept close watch over me.

Away we went through the woods that lined the east side of the road. It was bad walking, and with both my hands behind me I was several times in danger of stumbling. Indeed, once I did go down, but the firm grasp of my captors saved me from injury.

Presently we came to a long clearing, where it had once been the intention of some capitalists to build a railroad. But the matter had drifted into litigation, and nothing was done but to build a tool house and cut away the trees and brush.

The building had often been the resort of tramps, and was in a dilapidated condition. It was probably fifteen feet square, having a door at one end and a window at the other. The roof was flat and full of holes, but otherwise the building was fairly strong.

"Here we are, fellows," said Duncan, as we stopped in front of the door. "Just let go of him."

The others did as he requested. But they formed a small circle around me that I might not escape.

"Now that I have got you in a place free from interruption I intend to square up accounts with you," continued the president of the Models. "You hit me a foul blow this morning."

"You brought it on yourself, Duncan," I replied, as coolly as I could, though I was keenly interested.

"Stop! How many times must I tell you not to call me by my first name."

"Well, then, Woodward, if that suits you better."

"Mr. Woodward, if you please."

"Oh, come, Dunc, hurry up," interrupted Moran. "We don't want to stay here all day."

"I'm only teaching this fellow a lesson in politeness."

"All right; only cut it short."

"See here, Moran, who's the president of this club?"

"You are."

"Well, then, I'll take my own time," replied Duncan, loftily.

Edward Stratemeyer

"Go ahead then. But you'll have to do without me," rejoined Moran, considerably provoked by the other's domineering tone.

"I will?"

"Yes. I've got other things to do besides standing here gassing all day."

"Indeed!" sneered Duncan.

"Yes, indeed!"

I enjoyed the scene. It looked very much as if there would be lively times without my aid.

"You're getting up on your dignity mighty quick, Dan Moran."

"I don't intend to play servant-in-waiting for any one, Duncan Woodward."

"Who asked you to?"

" 'Actions speak louder than words.'"

"I'm the president of the Models, am I not?"

"Yes, but you're not a model president."

I could not help smiling at Moran's pun. He was not a bad chap, and had he not been to a great extent under Duncan's influence he might have been a first-rate fellow.

Of course, as is the fashion among men as well as boys, all the others groaned at the pun; and then Ellery broke in:—

"Come, come, this will never do. Go ahead with Strong, Dunc."

"I intend to," was the president's rejoinder. "But you all promised to stick by me, and I don't want any one to back out."

"I'm not backing out," put in Moran. "I only want to hurry matters up."

There was a pause after this speech, then Duncan addressed me:—

"Perhaps you are anxious to know why I brought you here?"

"Not particularly," I returned coldly.

Duncan gave a sniff.

"I guess that's all put on."

"Not at all. What I am anxious to know is, what you intend to do with me."

"Well, first of all I want you to get down on your knees and apologize for your conduct toward me this morning."

"Not much!" I cried.

"You are in my power."

"I don't care. Go ahead and do your worst," I replied recklessly, willing to suffer almost anything rather than apologize to such a chap as Duncan Woodward.

Besides, what had I done to call for an apology? I had

certainly treated him no worse than he deserved. He was a spoilt boy and a bully, and I would die rather than go down on my knees to him.

"You don't know what's in store for you," said Dunce, nonplussed by my manner.

"As I said before, I'll risk it."

"Very well. Where is the rope, boys?"

"Here you are," answered Pultzer. "Plenty of it."

As he spoke he produced a stout clothes line, five or six yards in length.

"We'll bind his hands a little tighter first," instructed Duncan, "and then his legs. Be sure and make the knots strong, so they won't slip. He must not escape us."

I tried to protest against these proceedings, but with my hands already bound it was useless.

In five minutes the clothes line had been passed around my body from head to feet, and I was almost as stiff as an Egyptian mummy.

"Now catch hold, and we'll carry him into the tool house," said Duncan. "I guess after he has spent twenty-four hours in that place without food or water he'll be mighty anxious to come to terms."

I was half dragged and half carried to the tool house and dropped upon the floor. Then the door was closed upon me, and I was left to my fate.

# CHAPTER IV

## THE TRAMP AGAIN

I am sure that all will admit that the prospect before me was not a particularly bright one. I was bound hand and foot and left without food or water.

Yet as I lay upon the hard floor of the tool house I was not so much concerned about myself as I was about matters at Widow Canby's house. It would be a hardship to pass the night where I was, to say nothing of how I might be treated when Duncan Woodward and his followers returned. But in the meantime, how would Kate fare?

I knew that my sister would be greatly alarmed at my continued absence. She fully expected me to be home long before this. As near as I could judge it was now an hour or so after noon, and she would have dinner kept warm on the kitchen stove, expecting every minute to see me drive up the lane.

Then again I was worried over the fact that the widow had left the house and her money in my charge. To be sure, the latter was locked up in her private secretary; but I felt it to be as much in my care as if it had been placed in my shirt bosom or the bottom of my trunk.

Edward Stratemeyer

I concluded that it was my duty, then, to free myself as quickly as possible from the bonds which the members of the Model Club had placed upon me. But this idea was more easily conceived than carried out.

In vain I tugged at the clothes line that held my arms and hands fast to my body. Duncan and the others had done their work well, and the only result of my efforts was to make the cord cut so deep into my flesh that several times I was ready to cry out from pain.

In my attempts I tried to rise to my feet, but found it an impossibility, and only succeeded in bumping my head severely against the wall.

There was no use in calling for help, and though I halloed several times I soon gave it up. I was fully three-quarters of a mile from any house and half that distance from the road, and who would be likely to hear me so far off?

The afternoon dragged slowly along, and finally the sun went down and the evening shadows crept up. By this time I was quite hungry and tremendously thirsty. But with nothing at hand to satisfy the one or allay the other I resolutely put all thoughts of both out of my head.

In the old tool house there had been left several empty barrels, behind which was a quantity of shavings that I found far more comfortable to rest upon than the bare floor.

As the evening wore on I wondered if I would be able to sleep. There was no use worrying about matters, as it would do no good, so I was inclined to treat the affair philosophically and make the best of it.

An hour passed, and I was just dropping into a light doze

when a noise outside attracted my attention. I listened intently and heard a man's footsteps.

I was inclined to call out, and, in fact, was on the point of so doing, when the door of the tool house opened and in the dim light I recognized the form of the tramp moulder who earlier in the day had so impudently asked me for help.

I was not greatly surprised to see him, for, as mentioned before, the old tool house was frequently used by men of his stamp. He had as much right there as I had, and though I was chagrined to see him enter I was in no position to protest.

On the contrary, I deemed it advisable to keep quiet. If he did not see me, so much the better. If he did, who could tell what indignities he might visit upon me?

So I crouched down behind the empty barrels, hardly daring to breathe. The man stumbled into the building, leaving the door wide open.

By his manner I was certain that he had been drinking heavily, and his rambling soliloquy proved it.

"The same old shebang," he mumbled to himself, as he swayed around in the middle of the floor, "the same old shebang where Aaron Woodward and I parted company four years ago. He's took care of his money, and I've gone to the dogs," and he gave a yawn and sat down on top of a barrel.

I was thoroughly surprised at his words. Was it possible that this seedy-looking individual had once been intimate with Duncan Woodward's father? It hardly seemed reasonable. I made a rapid calculation and concluded that the meeting must have had something to do with the proposed railroad in which I knew Mr. Woodward had held an interest. Perhaps this tramp had once been a prosperous contractor.

"Great times them were. Plenty of money and nothing to do," continued the man. "Wonder if any one in Darbyville would recognize—hold up, Stumpy, you mustn't repeat that name too often or you'll be mentioning it in public when it ain't no interest for you to do it. Stumpy, John Stumpy, is good enough for the likes of you."

And with great deliberation Mr. John Stumpy brought forth a short clay pipe which he proceeded to fill and light with evident satisfaction.

During the brief period of lighting up I caught a good glance at his face, and fancied that I saw beneath the surface of dirt and dissipation a look of shrewdness and intelligence. Evidently he was one of the unfortunates who allowed drink to make off with their brains.

Mr. John Stumpy puffed on in silence for several minutes. I wondered what he intended to do, and was not prepared for the surprises that were to follow.

"Times are changed and no mistake," he went on. "Here I am, down at the bottom, Nick Weaver dead, Woodward a rich man, and Carson Strong in jail. Humph! but times do change!"

Carson Strong! My heart gave a bound. This man was speaking of my father. What did it mean? What did the tramp know of the events of the past? As I lay behind the barrels, I earnestly hoped he would go on with his talk. I had heard just enough to arouse my curiosity.

I was certain that I had never, until that day, seen the man. What, then, could he have in common with my father?

Instinctively I connected the man with the cause of my father's imprisonment—I will not say downfall, because I firmly believed him innocent. Why I should do so I cannot to this day explain, but from the instant he mentioned my parent's name the man was firmly fixed in my memory.

In a few moments Mr. John Stumpy had puffed his pipe out, leaving the place filled with a heavy and vile smoke which gave me all I could do to keep from coughing. Then he slowly knocked the ashes from the bowl and restored the pipe to his pocket.

"Now I reckon I'm in pretty good trim to go ahead," he muttered as he arose. "No use of talking; there ain't anything like a good puff to steady a man's nerves. Was a time when I didn't need it, but them times are gone, and the least little job on hand upsets me. Wonder how much that old woman left behind."

I nearly uttered an ejaculation of astonishment. Was this man speaking of Mrs. Canby? What was the job that he contemplated?

Clearly there could be but one answer to that question. He knew the widow had gone away, and in her absence he contemplated robbing her house. Perhaps he had overheard her make mention of the money locked up in her desk, and the temptation to obtain possession of it was too strong to resist.

"I'll have to get rid of that boy and the dog, I suppose," he went on. "If it wasn't for the noise I'd shoot the dog; but it won't do to arouse the neighborhood. As for the lad, I reckon the sight of a pistol will scare him to death."

I was not so sure of that, and I grated my teeth at the thought

Edward Stratemeyer

of my present helplessness. Had I been free, I am sure I could have escaped easily, and perhaps have had the tramp arrested.

It was an alarming prospect. Kate was the only occupant of the house, and the nearest neighbor lived a full five hundred feet away. If attacked in the middle of the night, what would my sister do?

For a moment I felt like exposing myself, but then I reflected that such a course would not liberate me, and he would know that he had nothing to fear from me at the house, whereas, if I kept quiet, he might, by some lucky incident, be kept at bay.

So I lay still, wondering when he would start on his criminal quest.

"Now, one more drink and then I'll be off," he continued, and, producing a bottle, he took a deep draught. "Ha! That's the stuff to brace a man's nerves! But you mustn't drink too much, John Stumpy, or you'll be no good at all. If you'd only let liquor alone you might be as rich as Aaron Woodward, remember that." He gave something like a sigh. "Oh, well; let it pass. I'll get the tools and be on the way. The money in my pocket, I'll take the first train in the morning for the West." He paused a moment. "But no; I won't go until I've seen Woodward. He owes me a little on the old score, and I'll not go until he has settled up."

There was an interval of silence, during which Stumpy must have been feeling around in his pockets for a match; for a moment later there were several slight scratches, and then a tiny flame lit up the interior of the tool house.

"Let's see, where did I leave them tools? Ah, yes; I

remember now. Behind those barrels."

And Stumpy moved over to where I was in hiding.

# CHAPTER V

## FOLLOWING JOHN STUMPY

I expected to be discovered. I could not see how it could possibly be avoided. John Stumpy was but a few feet away. In a second more he would be in full sight of me.

What the outcome of the discovery would be I could not imagine. I was at the man's mercy, and I was inclined to think that, our interview of the morning would not tend to soften his feelings toward me.

But at that instant a small, yet extremely lucky incident occurred. A draught of wind came in at the partly open door and blew out the match, leaving the place in darkness.

"Confound the luck!" ejaculated John Stumpy, in high irritation. "There goes the light, and it's the last match I've got, too."

This bit of information was gratifying to me, and, without making any noise, I rolled back into the corner as far as possible.

"Well, I'll have to find them tools in the dark, that's all." He groped around for several seconds, during which I held my breath. "Ah, here they are, just as I left 'em last night. Reckon no one visits this shanty, and maybe it will be a good place to bring the booty, especially if I happen to be closely pushed."

I sincerely hoped that he would be closely pushed, and in fact so closely pushed that he would have no booty to bring. But if he did succeed in his nefarious plans, I was glad that I would know where to look for him.

No sooner had the man found the bag of tools,—which was nothing more nor less than a burglar's kit,—than he quitted the place, and I was left to my own reflections.

My thoughts alarmed me. Beyond a doubt John Stumpy intended to rob the Widow Canby's house. The only one at home was Kate, and I groaned as I thought of the alarm and terror that she might be called upon to suffer. As it was, I was sure she was worried about my continued absence. In my anguish I strove with all my might to burst asunder the bonds that held me. At the end of five minutes' struggle I remained as securely tied as ever.

What was to be done? It was a puzzling, but pertinent question. By hook or by crook I must get free. At great risk of hurting my head I rolled to the door of the tool house, which Stumpy had left wide open. Outside, the stars were shining brightly, and in the southwest the pale crescent of the new moon was falling behind the tree-tops, casting ghostly shadows that would have made a timid person shiver. But as the reader may by this time know, I was not of a timid nature, and I gave the shadows scant attention until a sudden movement among the trees attracted my notice. It was the figure of some person coming rapidly toward me.

At first I judged it must be Stumpy returning, and I was on

Edward Stratemeyer

the point of rolling back to my hiding-place when I saw that the newcomer was a boy.

When he reached the edge of the clearing he paused, and approached slowly.

"Roger Strong!" he called out. I instantly recognized the voice of Dick Blair, one of the youngest members of the Models, who, during my capture, had had little to say or do. He was the son of a wealthy farmer who lived but a short distance down the road from the Widow Canby's place.

I had always considered Dick a pretty good chap, and had been disagreeably surprised to see him in company with Duncan Woodward's crowd. How Duncan had ever taken up with him I could not imagine, except it might have been on account of the money Dick's father allowed him to have.

"Roger Strong!" he repeated. "Are you still here?"

I could, not imagine what had brought him to this place at such an hour of the night. Yet I answered at once.

"Yes, I am, Dick Blair."

"I thought maybe you had managed to get away," he continued, as he came closer.

"No; you fellows did your work pretty well," I replied as lightly as I could, for I did not want to show the white feather.

"Precious little I had to do with it," he went on, as he struck a match and lit a lantern that he carried.

"You were with the crowd."

"I know it; but I wouldn't have been if I'd known what they were up to. I hope you will not think too badly of me, Roger."

"I thought it was strange you would go into anything of this kind, Dick. What brings you back to-night?"

"I am ashamed of the whole thing," he answered earnestly, "and I came to release you—that is, on certain conditions."

My heart gave a bound. "What conditions, Dick?"

"I want you to promise that you won't tell who set you free," he explained. "If Dunc or the rest heard of it, they would never forgive me."

"What of it, Dick? Their opinion isn't worth anything."

"I know it—now. But they could tell mighty mean stories about me if they wanted to." And Dick Blair turned away and shuffled his foot on the ground to hide his shame.

"Don't mind them, Dick. If they start any bad report about you, do as I'm doing with the stain on our name—live it down."

"I'll try it. But you'll promise, won't you?"

"If you wish it, yes."

"All right; I know I can trust you," said Dick. Producing his pocket knife, he quickly cut the cords that bound me. Somewhat stiff from the position in which I had been forced to remain, I rose slowly to my feet.

"I don't know whether to thank you or not for what you've

done for me, Dick," I began. "But I appreciate your actions."

"I don't deserve any thanks. It was a mean trick, and I guess legally I was as guilty as any one. Just keep quiet about it and don't think too hard of me."

"I'll do both," I responded quickly.

"It's a mighty lonely place to spend the night in," he went on. "I'm no coward, but I wouldn't care to do it, all alone."

"I haven't been alone."

"No." And Dick looked intensely surprised. "Who has been here?"

I hesitated. Should I tell him?

"A tramp," I began.

"Why didn't he untie you?"

"He didn't see me."

"Oh, I suppose you hid away. What did he want, I wonder?"

"He was after some tools."

"Tools! There are none here, any more."

"But there were."

"What kind of tools?"

I hesitated again. Should I tell Dick the secret? Perhaps he might give me some timely assistance.

"Will you promise to keep silent if I tell?"

"Why, what do you mean, Roger?"

"It is very important."

"All right. Fire away."

"He came after some burglar's tools."

Dick stepped back in astonishment. "You surely don't mean it!" he gasped "Who was he going to rob?"

"The widow's house. He knows she is away and has left considerable money in her desk."

And in a rapid manner I told Dick of what I had overheard, omitting the mentioning of my father's and Mr. Woodward's names. Of course he was tremendously excited. What healthy country boy would not be?

"What are you going to do about it?" he questioned.

"Now I'm free I'm going to catch the fellow," I returned decidedly. "He shall not rob Mrs. Canby's house if I can help it."

"Aren't you afraid?"

"I intend to be cautious."

"He may have a pistol."

"The widow left one in the house. Maybe I can secure it. Then we'll be on an equal footing."

"I've got a pistol, Roger."

"You!"

"Yes, the Models all carry them. Dunc always insisted that it was the proper thing."

As Dick spoke, he produced a highly polished nickel-plated five-shooter.

"It looks like a good one," I said, after examining it. "Is it loaded?"

"Oh, yes; and I've got a box of cartridges in my pocket besides."

"Lend it to me, Dick."

"If you don't mind I'll—I'll go along with you, Roger," he returned. "You won't find me such a terrible coward."

"All right. But we must hurry. That fellow has got a good start, and he may even now be in the house."

"Hardly. He'll want to take a look around first."

Nevertheless, we lost no time in getting away from the tool house. We walked side by side, I with the pistol in the pocket of my jacket, and Dick with the lantern held aloft, that we might see to make rapid progress over the unaccustomed road.

It was a good walk to the widow's, and once Dick stumbled down in a heap, while the lantern rolled several yards away. But he picked himself up without grumbling and went along faster than ever.

"If I'm not mistaken, I saw that tramp down at the depot this morning," said he, as we drew near to the main road. "He was hanging around, and I thought he looked like a suspicious character."

"Did you see him yesterday?"

"No."

"Did you ever hear of him before?"

"I guess not. He was near the baggage room when I saw him. Then Mr. Woodward came up to see about a trunk, and the tramp made right off."

I was interested. John Stumpy had intimately that he intended to have an interview with Duncan Woodward's father, and if this was so, why had he not taken advantage of the opportunity thus offered?

I could arrive at but one conclusion. The tramp wished their meeting to be a strictly private one. He did not care to be seen in Mr. Woodward's presence, or else the wealthy merchant would not tolerate such a thing.

If the meeting was to be of a private nature, it would no doubt be of importance. Had my father's name not been mentioned I would not have cared; but as it was, I was deeply interested.

Perhaps it would be better to merely scare the fellow off. If he was captured, all chance of finding out his secrets might be lost.

By this time the reader may be aware that I thought John Stumpy's secrets important. Such was a fact. Try as hard as I was able, I could not but imagine that they concerned my father and his alleged downfall.

In five minutes Dick and I came within sight of Widow Canby's house. There was a light burning in the kitchen and another in the dining-room.

"Everything seems to be all right," said Dick, as we stood near a corner of the front fence. "I guess the fellow hasn't put in an appearance yet."

"I don't know. See I the side porch door is open. We gencrally keep it closed, and Kate would certainly have it shut if she was alone."

"What do you intend to do? Go into the house?"

"Guess we had better. I'd like to know where that fellow is," I replied. "Likely as not he is prowling about here some-where. If we can only catch sight of him, we can—Hark!"

As I uttered the last word, a shrill cry reached our ears. It was Kate's voice; and with my heart jumping wildly I made a dash for the house, with Dick Blair following me.

# CHAPTER VI

## A STRANGE ENVELOPE

I was sure that my sister's cry could mean but one thing—that the tramp had made a raid on the house. I was thoroughly alarmed, and ran with all possible speed in the direction of the dining-room, from whence the sound proceeded.

As I tore across the lawn, regardless of the bed of flowers which was Mrs. Canby's pride, Kate's cry was repeated, this time in a more intense tone. An instant later I dashed across the porch and into the room through the door that, as I have said, stood wide open.

I found my sister standing in the middle of the floor, holding in her hand a heavy umbrella with which she had evidently been defending herself. She was pale, and trembled from head to foot.

"What is it, Kate?" I exclaimed. "Where is the fellow?"

"Oh, Roger!" she gasped. "I'm so glad you've come. A tramp was here—he robbed—robbed the desk—the window—"

She pointed to the open window on the opposite side of the

Edward Stratemeyer

room. Then her breast heaved, the umbrella slipped from her grasp, and she sank into a chair.

"Are you hurt?" I cried anxiously.

"No, no—but the money—it is gone! What will Mrs. Canby say?"

And overcome with the dreadful thought, my sister fainted dead away.

As for myself I felt sick at heart. John Stumpy had been there—the widow's money had been stolen. What could be done?

Meanwhile, Dick Blair had come in. His common sense told him what had happened, and he set to work to restore my sister to consciousness.

"Will you stay here with Kate?" I asked.

"Certainly," he returned promptly. "But where are you going? After that tramp?"

"Yes."

"Be careful, for he may be a desperate character."

"I'm not afraid of him. I'm going to get that money back or know the reason why," was my determined reply; and I meant every word I said.

To my mind it was absolutely necessary that I recover the stolen property. It would have been bad enough to have had it taken when the Widow Canby was at home, but it had been stolen when left in my charge, and that was enough to make me turn Darbyville district up side down before letting the matter drop.

Besides, there was still another important factor in the case. I knew well enough that if the money was not recovered, there would be plenty of people mean enough to intimate that I had had something to do with its disappearance. The Strong honor was considered low by many, and they would not hesitate to declare that I was only following in my father's footsteps.

To a person already suffering under an unjust accusation such an intimation is doubly stinging, and when I told Dick that I was not afraid of Mr. John Stumpy, I meant that I would rather face the robber now than the Darbyville people later on.

"I want to take the pistol," I added.

"All right. There is the box of extra cartridges. Do you want the lantern?"

"Yes; I may want to use it before I return. I'll blow it out now."

Our conversation had lasted but a few seconds, and an instant after I was on my way, the lantern on my left arm and the pistol in my right hand.

"Take good care of Kate," I called back as I passed out.

"I will," replied Dick. "Don't stay away too long, if you don't find the fellow."

I passed around to the other side of the garden, where an open gateway led to the pear orchard. I felt pretty certain that

John Stumpy had pursued this course, and I entered the orchard on a run.

The thief, I reckoned, was not over five minutes ahead of me. To be sure, he could easily hide, but it was not likely that he would care to remain in the neighborhood, unless it was really necessary for him to see Mr. Aaron Woodward.

When I got well into the orchard, where it was darker than in the garden, I listened intently, hoping that I might hear some sound that would guide me.

But all was silent. Occasionally a night bird fluttered through the trees and a frog gave a dismal croak, but otherwise not a sound broke the stillness.

I continued on my way toward the road, and reaching the fence, paused again.

Had the thief jumped over? If so, which way had he gone, up, down, or into the woods beyond? It was a perplexing question. Perhaps if I had been in a story book I might have found some clew to direct me. But I was not that kind of a hero. I was only an everyday boy, and consequently no clew presented itself.

I stood by the fence for several minutes, my eyes and ears on the alert to catch anything worthy of notice. I judged it was near midnight, and hardly had I thought of the matter before the distant town bells tolled the hour of twelve.

As the echo of the last stroke died away, two figures came slowly up the road. As they drew nearer, I recognized Moran and Pultzer, the two Models members who had assisted at my capture.

I was astonished at their appearance. What on earth could they be doing out at this time of night?

As they drew near I thought for many reasons that it would not be advisable to show myself, and I stepped behind a tree.

"I don't care what you say," said Pultzer, "Dunc was half scared to death when we came away."

"I guess he didn't think what a serious matter it was when he asked us to go into it," returned Moran. "It's the worst affair I ever got into."

"Ditto myself," responded Pultzer.

"And if we get out without being caught, you'll never find me in another such," continued the other earnestly.

"I wonder what Dunc's father will say when he hears of it?"

"And all the rest of the Darbyville people? Of course they've got to lay it to some one."

I surmised that they must be speaking of what they had done to me. I never dreamed that they were discussing a subject much more serious.

"I'm glad Dick Blair wasn't along to-night," went on Moran. "Dick is not to be trusted any more. He kicked awfully at the idea of tying up Strong this noon."

I was gratified to hear this bit of news. I liked Dick in many respects, and now I was almost ready to look upon him as a friend.

"Strong didn't give in quite as much as Dunc thought he

would. Hang it, if I didn't admire his grit."

"So did I. Wonder how he's getting along in the old tool house. We must release him first thing in the morning."

"No need of doing that, gentlemen," I put in, stepping out from behind the tree. "I am—"

But it would have been useless for me to say more, as no one would have heard me.

At the first sound of my voice both of the Models had started in alarm, and then, led by Pultzer, they dashed up the road as fast as their feet could carry them.

At first I was amazed at their actions, and then, as the ridiculousness of the situation presented itself, I smiled. "A guilty conscience needeth no accuser," it is said, and this truth was verified to the letter.

Yet I was sorry that I had not had a chance to speak to them. I wanted to question them in regard to the thief. Perhaps they had seen him, and if so, I did not want to miss my chance of getting upon his track.

Jumping over the fence, I walked slowly down the road, but not in hopes of meeting John Stumpy. If he was anywhere near, the approach of the two boys had certainly driven him into hiding.

Suddenly I thought of the tool house. The tramp had spoken of returning to the place. He evidently knew the road. I determined to go to the spot and make a search at once.

It was no easy matter to find my way back to the tool house, and at the risk of being seen I lit the lantern.

As I walked along I wondered how my sister and Dick were faring. No doubt Kate had been much surprised to see who was with her on her recovery, and I sincerely hoped that the shock Stumpy had given her would not have any evil effects. She was a sensitive girl, and such happenings were calculated to try her nerves severely.

At length I came within sight of the clearing. Here I hesitated for an instant, and then, pistol in hand, approached the tool house boldly.

The door was still open, and I entered, only to find the place empty.

With a sigh I realized that my journey thither was a useless one. Nothing remained but to go back to the road, and I was about to leave again when the rays of the lantern fell upon a white object lying on the floor.

I picked it up. It was a common square envelope. Thinking it contained a letter I turned it over to read the address. Judge of my astonishment when I read the following:—

Dying Statement of Nicholas Weaver Concerning the Forgeries for which Carson Strong Was Sent to State's Prison.

# CHAPTER VII

## A WAR OF WORDS

No words of mine can express the feeling that came over me as I read the superscription written on the envelope I had picked up in the old tool house.

Was it possible that this envelope contained the solution of the mystery that had taken away our good name and sent my father to prison? The very thought made me tremble.

The packet was not a thick one. In fact, it was so thin that for an instant I imagined the envelope was empty. But a hasty examination proved my fears groundless.

In nervous excitement I put the lantern down on the top of a barrel, and then drew from the envelope the single shoot of foolscap that it contained. A glance showed me that the pages were closely written in a cramped hand extremely difficult to read.

For the moment I forgot everything else—forgot that the Widow Canby's house had been robbed and that I was on the track of the robber—and drawing close to the feeble light the lantern afforded, strove with straining eyes and palpitating heart to decipher the contents of the written pages.

"I, Nicholas Weaver, being on the point of death from pneumonia, do make this my last statement, which I hereby swear is true in every particular."

This was the beginning of the document which I hoped would in some way free my father's character from the stain that now rested on it.

Exactly who Nicholas Weaver was I did not know, though it ran in my mind that I had heard this name mentioned by my father during the trial.

Beyond the opening paragraph I have quoted the handwriting was almost illegible, and in the dim light it was only here and there that I could pick out such words as "bank," "assumed," "risk," "name," and so forth, which gave but an inkling of the real contents of the precious document.

"It's too bad," was my thought. "I'd give all I possess to be able to read this right off, word for word."

Hardly had the reflection crossed my mind when a noise outside startled me. I had just time enough to thrust the paper into my pocket when the door was swung open and the tramp appeared.

He was evidently as much surprised as I was, for he stopped short in amazement, while the short pipe he carried between his lips fell unnoticed to the floor.

I rightly conjectured he had not noticed the light of the lantern and fully believed the tool house tenantless.

"You here!" he cried.

"It looks like it, doesn't it?" was all I could find to reply, and as I spoke my hand sought the pistol I carried.

"What brought you here?" he demanded roughly.

"I came after you," I returned as coolly as I could; and by this time I had the pistol where it could be brought into instant use.

"What do you want of me?"

"I want you to hand over the money you stole awhile ago."

"What are you talking about? I never stole any money."

"You did. You broke into the Widow Canby's house less than an hour ago. Come, hand over that money."

The fellow gave a coarse laugh. "Ha! ha! do you think I'm to be bluffed by a boy? Get home with you, before I hammer you for calling me a thief."

"That's just what you are, and I don't intend to go until you hand over the money, John Stumpy," I returned decidedly.

"Ha! you know my name?"

I bit my lip. I was sorry for the slip I had made. But I put on a bold front. "I know what you are called," I replied.

"What I am called?"

"Yes."

"What do you mean? Come, out with it."

"I will when I please. In the meantime hand over that money."

"You talk like a fool!" he cried.

"Never mind. You'll find I won't act like one."

"What do you know about me?" he went on curiously, believing, no doubt, that he was perfectly safe from attack.

"I know more than you think. I know you are a burglar, and may be worse."

"I'll kill you!" he cried, rushing forward.

"Stand where you are!" I returned, pulling out the pistol. "Don't stir a step."

He did not see the weapon until he was fairly upon me. The glint of the nickeled steel made him shiver.

"Don't shoot!" he cried in sudden terror, that showed he was a coward at heart. "Don't—don't shoot."

"I won't if you do as I tell you."

"Do what?"

"Give up the widow's money."

"See here, young fellow, you've made a mistake. I never was near the widow's house, 'cepting this morning."

"I know better. You just broke open her desk and stole over two hundred dollars."

"It's a mistake. Put down the pistol and I'll tell you all about it."

"I'm not such a fool, Mr. John Stumpy, or whatever your name is," was my decided reply.

The tone of my voice disconcerted the man, for he paused as if not knowing what to say next.

"Say, young feller, do you want to make some money?" he asked suddenly, after a short pause.

The change in his manner surprised me.

"How?" I asked, although I knew about what was coming.

"I've got nearly three hundred dollars in cash with me. I'll give you fifty of it if you'll go home and say you couldn't find me."

"Thank you; I'm not doing business that way," I rejoined coldly.

"Fifty dollars ain't to be sneezed at," he went on insinuatingly.

"I wouldn't care if you offered me fifty thousand," I cried sharply. "I'm no thief."

"Humph; don't you suppose I know who you are?" he went on. "You're the son of a thief. Do you hear that?—the son of a thief! What right have you got to set yourself up to be any better than your father was afore you?"

"Take care!" I cried, my blood fairly boiling as I spoke. He saw his mistake.

"I didn't mean no harm, partner. But what's the use of being high toned when it don't pay?"

"It always pays to be honest," I said firmly.

"There are those who don't think so any more than I," he replied.

"My father never was a thief. They may say all they please, I will always think him innocent."

"Humph!"

"If it hadn't been for men like you and Nicholas Weaver, my father would never be in prison."

The words were out before I knew it. They were most injudicious ones.

"What do you mean?" gasped the man. "What do you know about Nick Weaver?"

"More than you imagine. When he died he made a confession—"

"It's false. Nick Weaver wasn't in his right mind when he died, anyhow."

"Perhaps he was."

"What you—" began the man. Then he paused and began a rapid search in his pockets. "You've got that paper," he cried hoarsely. "Give it up," and as he spoke, John Stumpy took a threatening step toward me.

"Stand back!" and I raised the pistol.

I was trembling in every limb, but I actually believe I would have fired it if he had rushed upon me.

"I won't. Give up that paper."

"Never. I'll die first."

And die I would. His earnestness convinced me of the letter's worth. If it contained that which could clear my father's name, only death would be the means of parting me from it.

"Give it up, I say! Do you think I'm to be defeated by a boy?"

"Stand back!"

I raised the pistol on a level with his head. As I did so, he made a dash forward and caught up a stick which was lying near.

"I'll fix you!" he roared, and swinging the billet over his head, he brought it down with all his force on my arm, causing the pistol to fly from my hand into a corner beyond.

"Now we'll see who's master here," he cried exultingly. "You're a smart boy, but you don't know everything!" Rushing over to the corner, he secured the pistol and aimed it at me. "Now, we'll settle this matter according to my notions," he went on triumphantly.

# CHAPTER VIII

## THE STRUGGLE

I was deeply chagrined at the unexpected turn affairs had taken, and I felt decidedly uncomfortable as John Stumpy levelled the weapon at my head. I could readily see that the battle of words was at an end. Action was now the order of the day. I wondered what the fellow would do next; but I was not kept long in suspense.

"Now, it's my turn, young fellow," he remarked, with a shrewd grin, as I fell back.

"Well, what do you want?" I asked, as coolly as I could recognizing the fact that nothing was to be gained by "stirring him up."

"You'll see fast enough. In the first place, hand over that paper."

I was silent. I did not intend to tell a falsehood by saying I did not have it, nor did I intend to give it up if it could possibly be avoided.

"Did you hear what I said?" continued Stumpy, after a pause.

Edward Stratemeyer

"I thought you said the paper wasn't valuable," I returned, more to gain time than anything else.

"Neither it ain't, but, just the same, I want it. Come, hand it over."

He was getting ugly now, and no mistake. What was to be done?

As I have mentioned before, it would have been useless to call for help, as no one would have heard the calls.

Suddenly the thought struck me to try a bit of deception. I put my hand in my pocket and drew out the empty envelope.

"Is that what you want?" I asked, holding it up.

"Reckon it is," he returned eagerly. "Just toss it over."

Somewhat disappointed that he did not approach me and thus give me a chance of attacking him, I did as requested. It fell at his feet, and he was not long in transferring it to his pocket.

"Next time don't try to walk over a man like me," he said sharply. "I know a thing or two, and I'm not to be downed by a boy."

"Are you satisfied?" I asked calmly, though secretly exultant that he had not discovered my trick.

"Not yet. You followed me when you had no business to, and now you've got to take the consequences."

"What are you going to do?"

"You'll see soon enough. I ain't the one to make many mistakes. Years ago I made a few, but I ain't making no more."

"You knew my father quite well, didn't you?" I inquired in deep curiosity.

"As the old saying goes, 'Ask me no questions and I'll tell you no lies.' Maybe I didn't; maybe I did."

"I know you did."

"Well, what of it? So did lots of other people."

"But not quite as well as you and Nicholas Weaver and Mr. Aaron Woodward," I continued, determined to learn all I could.

"Ha! What do you know of them?" He scowled at me. "Reckon you've been reading that paper of Nick's putty closely. I was a fool for not tearing it up long ago."

"Why did you keep it—to deliver it to Mr. Wentworth?"

It was a bold stroke and it told. Stumpy grew pale in spite of the dirt that covered his face, and the hand that held the pistol trembled.

"Say, young fellow, you know too much, you do. I suppose you read that paper clear through, did you?"

"As you say: Maybe I didn't; maybe I did."

"Perhaps you wasn't careful of it. Maybe I'd better examine it," he added.

My heart sank within me. In another moment the deception I had practised would be known—and then?

He fumbled in his pocket and drew forth the envelope. He could not extract the letter he supposed it contained with one hand very well, and so lowered the pistol for a moment.

This was my chance. Unarmed I was evidently in his power. If I could only escape from the tool house!

The door still stood partly open, and the darkness of night—for the moon had gone down—was beyond. A dash and I would be outside. Still the tramp stood between me and liberty. Should I attack him or endeavor to slip to one side?

I had but an instant to think; another, and it would be too late. John Stumpy was fumbling in the envelope. His eyes were searching for the precious document.

With a single bound I sprang against him, knocking him completely off his feet. Then I made another jump for the door.

But he was too quick for me. Dropping the envelope and the pistol, he caught me by the foot, and in an instant both of us were rolling on the floor.

It was an unequal struggle. Strong as I was for a boy of my age, I was no match for this burly man. Turn and twist all I could, he held me in his grip while he heaped loud imprecations upon my head.

In our movements on the floor we came in contact with the lantern and upset it, smashing the frame as well as the glass.

For a moment darkness reigned. Then a tiny light from the

corner lit up the place. The flames had caught the shavings.

"The place is on fire!" I cried in horror.

"Yes, and you did it," replied the tramp.

"It was you!" I returned stoutly, and, as a matter of fact, it may be as well to state that John Stumpy's foot had caused the accident.

"Not much; it was your fault, and you've got to take the blame."

As the rascal spoke, he caught me by the throat, squeezing it so tightly that I was in great danger of being choked to death.

"Let—let up!" I gasped.

The choking continued. My head began to grow dizzy, and strange lights danced before my eyes. I protested against this proceeding as vigorously as I could by kicking the man sharply and rapidly.

But Stumpy now meant to do me real injury. He realized that I knew too much for his future welfare. In fact, he, no doubt, imagined I knew far more than I really did. If I was out of the way for all time so much the better for him.

"Take that!" he suddenly cried, and springing up he brought his heel down with great force on my head.

I cannot describe the sensation that followed. It was as if a sharp, blinding pain had stung me to the very heart. Then my senses forsook me.

How long I lay in a comatose state I do not know. Certainly

it could not have been a very long time—probably not over five or six minutes.

In the meantime the fire rapidly spread igniting the barrels that were stored in the tool house, and climbing up the walls of the building to the roof.

When I recovered my senses, my face was fairly scorched, and no sooner had I opened my eyes than they were blinded by smoke and flame.

By instinct rather than reason I staggered to my feet. I was so weak I could hardly stand, and my head spun around like a top. Where was the door?

I tottered to one side and felt around. There was the window tightly closed. The door I knew was opposite.

Reeling, I made my way through the smoke that now seemed to fill my lungs, to where I knew the door to be. Oh, horror! it was closed and secured!

"Heaven help me now!" burst from my parched lips. "Am I to be roasted alive?"

With all my remaining strength I threw myself against the door. Once, and again, and still it did not budge.

"Help! help!" I called at the top of my voice.

No answer came to my cry. The fire behind me became hotter and hotter. The roof had now caught, and the sparks fell down upon me in a perfect shower.

Another moment and it would be all over. With a brief prayer to God for help in my dire need, I attacked the door for the last time.

At first it did not budge. Then there was a creaking, a sharp crack, and at last it flew wide open.

Oh, how grateful was the breath of fresh air that struck me! I stumbled out into the clearing and opened wide my throat to take in the pure draught.

Then for the first time I realized how nearly I had been overcome. I could no longer stand, and swooning, sank in a heap to the ground.

Edward Stratemeyer

# CHAPTER IX

## NEW TROUBLE

"He's alive, boys."

These were the words that greeted my ears on recovering my senses. I opened my eyes and saw that I was surrounded by a number of boys and men.

"How did you come here?" asked Henry Morse, a sturdy farmer who lived in the neighborhood.

I was too much confused to make any intelligent reply. Rising to a sitting position, I gazed around.

The tool house had burned to the ground, there being no means at hand to extinguish the fire. The glare of the conflagration had called out several dozens of people from Darbyville and the vicinity, several of whom had stumbled upon me as I lay in the clearing.

"What's the matter, Roger?" asked Larry Simpson, a young man who kept a bookstore in the town.

"The matter is that I nearly lost my life in that fire," I replied.

"How did you come here?"

As briefly as I could I related my story, leaving out all references to my personal affairs and the finding of Nicholas Weaver's statement. At present I considered it would do no good to disclose what I knew on those points.

"I think I saw that tramp yesterday," said Larry after I had finished. "He bought a sheet of paper and an envelope in my store, and then asked if he could write a letter there."

"And did he?" I asked in curiosity.

"Yes. At first I hated to let him do it,—he looked so disreputable,—but then I thought it might be an application for a position, and so told him to go ahead."

"Who did he write to? do you know?"

"Somebody in Chicago, I think."

"Do you remember the name?"

"He tried the pen on a slip of paper first. It wouldn't work very well. But I think the name was Holtzmann, or something similar."

I determined to remember the name, thinking it might prove of value sometime.

"The thing of it is," broke in Henry Morse, "what has become of this Stumpy? If he stole the Widow Canby's money, it's high time somebody was after him."

"That's true," ejaculated another. "Have you any idea which way the fellow went?"

Of course I had not. Indeed, I was hardly in condition to do any rational thinking, much less form an opinion. The thief might be in hiding close at hand, or he might be miles away.

"Some of us had better make a search," put in another. "Come, boys, we'll spread out and scour the woods."

"That's a good idea," said Tony Parsons, the constable of the town. "Meanwhile, Roger Strong, let us go to Judge Penfold's house and put the case in his hands. He'll get out a warrant, and perhaps a reward."

I thought this was a good idea, and readily assented, first, however, getting one of the boys to promise that he would call at the widow's house and quiet Kate's fears concerning my whereabouts.

It was now early morning, and we had no difficulty in making our way through the woods to the main road.

"Guess we won't find the judge up yet," remarked Tony Parsons as we hurried along. "I've never yet found him out of bed afore seven o'clock. It will make him mighty mad to get up afore this time."

"I'm sorry to disturb him," I replied, with something of awe at the thought of rousing a magistrate of the law.

"But it's got to be done," went on Parsons, with a grave shake of his head, "unless we all want to be murdered and robbed in our beds!"

"That's true. I'd give all I'm worth to catch that tramp."

"Reckon Widow Canby'll be dreadfully cut up when she hears about the robbery."

"I suppose so."

"She may blame you, Roger. You see if it was anybody else, it would be different. But being as it's you, why—"

"I know what you mean," I returned bitterly. "No one in Darbyville believes I can be honest."

"I ain't saying nothing against you, Roger," returned Parsons, hastily. "I reckon you ain't no worse than any other boy. But you know what public sentiment is."

"So I do; but public sentiment isn't always right," was my spirited answer.

"Who did you say those boys were that tied you up?" went on the constable, to change the subject.

"Duncan Woodward was the principal one."

"Phew! Reckon he didn't think tying you up would prove such a serious matter."

"If it hadn't been for that, the robbery might have been prevented. I would have been home guarding the widow's property, as she expected me to do."

"Reckon so you would."

"In a certain sense I hold Duncan Woodward and his followers responsible for what has occurred."

"Phew! What will Mr. Woodward say to that, I wonder?"

"I can't help what he says. I'm not going to bear all the blame when it isn't my fault."

"No, neither would I."

At length we reached the outskirts of the town. Judge Penfold lived at the top of what was termed the Hill, the aristocratic district of the place, and thither we made our way.

"Indeed, but the judge ain't stirring yet!" exclaimed the Irish girl who came to answer our summons at the door.

"Then wake him at once," said Parsons. "Tell him there has been a most atrocious robbery and assault committed."

"Mercy on us!" said the girl, lifting up her hands in horror. "And who was it, Mr. Parsons?"

"Never mind who it was. Go at once."

"I will that! Robbery and assault. Mercy on us!"

And leaving us standing in the hall, the hired girl sped up the front stairway.

"The judge will be down as soon as he can," she reported on her return.

We waited as patiently as we could. While doing so I revolved what had occurred over in my mind, and came to the conclusion that the crime would be a difficult one to trace. John Stumpy had probably made good use of his time, knowing that even if I had lost my life in the fire my sister would still recognize him as the thief.

Suddenly I thought of the written confession that must yet remain in my pocket, and I was on the point of assuring myself that it was still safe when a heavy foot-step sounded overhead, and Judge Penfold came down.

The judge was a tall, slender men of fifty, with hollow cheeks, a pointed nose, and a sharp chin. His voice was of a peculiarly high and rasping tone, and his manner far from agreeable.

"What's the trouble?" he demanded, and it was plain to see that he did not relish having his early morning sleep broken.

"Widow Canby's house was robbed last night," replied the constable; and he gave the particulars.

Judge Penfold was all ears at once. Indeed, it may be as well to state that he was a widower and had paid Widow Canby much attention, which, however, I well knew that good lady heartily resented. No doubt he thought if he could render her any assistance it would help along his suit.

"We must catch the fellow at once," he said. "Parsons, you must catch him without fail."

"Easier said than done, judge," replied the constable, doubtfully. "Where am I to look for him? The country around here is pretty large."

"No matter. You are constable, and it is your duty to seek him out. I will sign the warrant for his arrest, and you must have him in jail by to-night, without fail."

"I'll do what I can, judge," returns Parsons, meekly.

"Strong, I'll have to bind you over as a witness."

"Bind me over?" I queried in perplexity. "What do you mean?"

"Hold you, unless you can give a bond to appear when wanted."

"But I had nothing to do with the burglary."

"You are principal accuser of this John Stumpy."

"Well, I'll promise to be on hand whenever wanted."

"That is not sufficient. Your character is—is not—ahem! of the best, and—"

"Why is my character not of the best?" I demanded.

"Well, ahem! Your father, you see—"

"Is innocent."

"Perhaps—perhaps, but, nevertheless, I will have to hold you. Parsons, I will leave him in your charge."

"You have no right to arrest me," I cried, for I knew very little of the law.

"What's that?" demanded Judge Penfold, pompously. "You forget I am the judge of that."

"I don't care," I burst out. "I have done no wrong."

"It ain't that, Roger. Many innocent men are held as witnesses," put in Parsons.

"But I've got to attend to Mrs. Canby's business," I explained.

"I fancy Mrs. Canby would rather get on the track of her

money," said Judge Penfold severely. "Can you furnish bail?"

I did not know that I could. The woman who had been robbed was my only friend, and she was away.

"Then you'll have to take him to the lockup, Parsons."

This news was far from agreeable. It would be no pleasant thing to be confined in the Darbyville jail, not to say anything of the anxiety it might cause Kate. Besides, I wanted to follow up John Stumpy. I was certain I could do it fully as well as the constable.

"Come, Roger, there is no help for it," said Parsons, as I still lingered. "It's the law, and it won't do any good to kick."

"Maybe not, but, nevertheless, it isn't fair."

We walked out into the front hall, the judge following us.

"Of course if you can get bail any time during the day I will let you go," he said; "I will be down in my office from nine to twelve and two to four."

"Will you offer a reward for the capture of the man?" I asked.

"I cannot do that. The freeholders of the county attend to all such matters. Parsons, no doubt, will find the scoundrel."

As the judge finished there was a violent ringing of the door bell. Judge Penfold opened the door and was confronted by Mr. Aaron Woodward, who looked pale and excited.

"Judge, I want you—hello! that boy! Judge, I want that boy

arrested at once! Don't you let him escape!"

"Want me arrested?" I ejaculated in astonishment. "What for?"

"You know well enough. You thought to hide your tracks, but I have found you out. Parsons, don't let him get out of the door. He's a worse villain than his father was!"

# CHAPTER X

## UNDER ARREST

I will not hesitate to state that I was nearly stunned by Mr. Aaron Woodward's unexpected statement. I knew that when he announced that I was a worse villain than my father he meant a good deal.

Yet try as hard as I could it was impossible for me to discover what he really did mean. I was not conscious of having done him any injury, either bodily or otherwise. Indeed, of late I had hardly seen the man. The Widow Canby was not partial to dealings with him, and I never went near him on my own account.

It was plain to see that the merchant was thoroughly aroused. His face was pale with anger, and the look he cast upon me was one of bitter resentment. For the instant he eyed me as if he intended to spring upon me and choke the life out of my body, and involuntarily I shrank back. But then I recollected that the minions of the law who stood beside me would not allow such a course of procedure, and this made me breathe more freely.

"Yes, sir; he's a worse villain than his father!" repeated Mr. Aaron Woodward, turning to Judge Penfold; "a most

Edward Stratemeyer

accomplished villain, sir." And he shook his fist within an inch of my nose.

"What have I done to you, Mr. Woodward?" I demanded, as soon as I could speak.

"Done, sir? You know very well what you've done, you young rascal!" puffed the merchant. "Oh, but I'll make you pay dearly for your villainy."

"I've committed no villainy," I returned warmly. "If you refer to the way I treated Duncan this morning, why all I've got to say is that it was his own fault, and I can prove it."

"Treated Duncan? Oh, pshaw! This is far more serious affair than a boy's quarrel. Don't let him escape, Parsons"—the last to the constable, who had his hand on my shoulder.

"No fear, sir," was Parson's reply. "He's already under arrest."

"Under arrest?" repeated the merchant quickly. "Then you've already heard—"

"He is ahem—only under detention as a witness," spoke up Judge Penfold. "I do not think he had anything to do with the theft of the widow's money."

"Widow's money! What do you mean?"

In a few words Judge Penfold explained the situation. "Isn't this what you came about?" he asked then.

"Indeed, no, sir. My affair is far more important—at least to me. But you can make up your mind that Strong's story is purely fiction. He is undoubtedly the real culprit, undoubtedly. Takes after his father."

"My father was an honest man!" I cried out. "I don't care what you or any one may say! Some day he will be cleared of the stain on his name."

"Oh, undoubtedly," sneered Mr. Woodward. "Mean while, however, the community at large had better keep a sharp eye on his son. Whom do you assert stole the Widow Canby's money?"

"A tramp."

"Humph! A likely story."

"It's true. His name was John Stumpy."

"John Stumpy!"

As Mr. Aaron Woodwind uttered the name, all the color forsook his face.

"Yes, sir. And he claimed to know you," I went on, my curiosity amused over the merchant's show of feeling.

"It's a falsehood! I never heard of such a man," cried Mr. Woodward, but his face belied his words.

"Well, what is your charge against Strong?" asked Judge Penfold, impatiently, probably tired of being so utterly ignored in the discussion.

The merchant hesitated.

"I prefer to speak to you about the matter in private," he said sourly.

Edward Stratemeyer

"That isn't fair. He ought to tell me what I am accused of," I cried, "Every one who is arrested has a right to know that. I have done no wrong and I am not afraid."

"All assumed bravery, Judge Penfold; quite assumed, sir."

"No, sir. Tell me why you want me locked up," I repeated.

But instead of replying Mr. Woodward drew Judge Penfold to the rear end of the hall and began to speak in so low a tone that I could not catch a word.

"You don't mean it!" I heard the judge say presently. "Come into the library and give me the particulars."

The two men passed into the room, closing the door tightly behind them. They were gone nearly quarter of an hour—a long wait for me. I wondered what could be the nature of Mr. Woodward's accusation against me, but failed to solve the mystery.

At length they came out. Judge Penfold's face was a trifle sterner than before. Mr. Woodward looked pleased, as if his argument had proven conclusive.

"You will take Strong to the jail at once," said the judge to Parsons "and tell Booth to be careful of his prisoner."

"Yes, sir."

"Don't let him escape," added Aaron Woodward, anxiously. "Don't let him escape, sir, under any circumstances."

"No fear," was Parsons's ready answer. "I never had one of 'em give me the slip yet."

And with great gravity he drew from his pocket a pair of ancient handcuffs, one of which he attached to my wrist and the other to his own.

"Come, Roger. Better take it easy," he said. "No use of kicking. March!"

"But I'd like to know something about this," I protested. "What right—"

"It is all quite legal," put in Judge Penfold, pompously. "I understand the law perfectly."

"But—"

"Say no more. Parsons, take him away."

"I shall see you later," whispered Mr. Woodward in my ear as the constable hurried me off.

The next instant we were on the street. Arrests in Darbyville were rare, and by the time we reached the jail we had a goodly following of boys and idle men, all anxious to know what was up.

"He stole the Widow Canby's money," I heard one man whisper, to which another replied:—

"Light fingered, eh? Must take after his father. I always knew the Strongs couldn't be trusted."

The jail was a small affair, being nothing more than the loft over a carpenter shop. The jailer was a round-faced man named Booth, who filled in his spare time by doing odd jobs of carpentering in the shop downstairs. We found him hard at work glueing some doors together. I knew him tolerably

Edward Stratemeyer

well, and he evinced considerable surprise at seeing me in custody.

"What, Roger; arrested! What for?"

"That's what I would like to know," I returned.

In a few words Parsons told him what was to be done, and Booth led the way upstairs.

"'Tain't a very secure place," he returned. "Reckon I'll have to nail down some of the windows unless you'll give me your word not to run away."

"I'll promise nothing," was my reply. "I'm being treated unfairly, and I shall do as I think best."

"Then I'll fasten everything as tight as a drum," returned Booth.

Going below, he secured a hammer and some nails, with which he secured the windows and the scuttle on the roof.

"Reckon it's tight enough now," he said. "Just wait, Parsons, till I get him a bucket of water."

This was done, and then the two men left me, closing and locking the door of the enclosed staircase behind them.

The loft was empty, saving a nail keg that stood in one corner of the floor. Pulling this out, I sat down to think matters over.

Try my best I could not imagine what charge Mr. Aaron Woodward had brought against me. Yet such had been his earnestness that for the nonce everything else was driven from my mind.

The sounds of talking below interrupted my meditations. I recognized Kate's voice, and the next moment my sister stood beside me.

"Oh, Roger!" was all she could say, and catching me by the arm she burst into tears.

"Don't take it so hard, Kate," I said. "Make sure it will all come out right in the end."

"But to be arrested like—like a thief! Oh, Roger, it is dreadful!"

"Never mind. I have done no wrong, and I'm not afraid of the result. Have they heard anything of John Stumpy yet?"

"Dick Blair says not. Mr. Parsons and the rest are after him, but he seems to have disappeared for good—and Mrs. Canby's money with him."

"Have you heard from her yet?"

"No; but I've written her a letter and just posted it to Norfolk."

"She won't get it till day after to-morrow."

"What will she say? Oh, Roger, do you think—"

"No, I don't. The widow always trusted me, and I know she'll take my word now. She is not so narrow-minded as the very folks who look down on her."

"But it is awful! Over two hundred dollars! We can never

make it up. We've only got twenty-eight!"

"We can't exactly be called upon to make it up—" I began.

"But we'll want to," put in Kate, hastily.

"I'd feel better if we did. The widow has always been so kind to us."

"How long must you stay here?"

"I don't know. As long as Judge Penfold sees fit, I suppose."

"If only they could catch this John Stumpy."

"I hope so—for other reasons than those you know, Kate."

"Other reasons?"

"Yes; very important ones, too. John Stumpy knew father well. And he was mixed up in that—that miserable affair."

"Oh, Roger, how do you know?"

"I heard him say so. Besides, he dropped a letter that proved it. I have the letter in my pocket now. It's the dying statement of one Nicholas Weaver—"

"Nicholas Weaver! He was a clerk with father!"

"So I thought. Who Stumpy is, though, I don't know. Do you?"

"No; but his face I'm sure I've seen before. Let me see the letter. Have you read it?"

"No; I hadn't time to spell it out, it is so badly written. Maybe you can read it."

"I'll try," replied Kate. "Hand it over."

I put my hand in my pocket to do so. The statement was gone!

# CHAPTER XI

## AARON WOODWARD'S VISIT

Puzzled and dismayed, I made a rapid search of my clothes—first one pocket and then another. It was useless. Beyond a doubt the statement was nowhere about my person.

I was quite sure it had not been taken from me. Strange as it may seem, neither Parsons nor Booth had searched me. Perhaps they deemed it useless to take away the possessions of a poor country boy. My jack-knife and other odds and ends were still in their accustomed places.

"It's gone!" I gasped, when I was certain that such was a fact.

"Gone?" repeated Kate.

"Yes, gone, and I don't know where. They didn't take it from me. I must have lost it."

"Oh, Roger, and it was so important!"

"I know it, Kate. It must have dropped from my pocket down at the tool house. Perhaps if I go down I can find it."

"Go down?" she queried.

"Oh, I forgot I was a prisoner."

"Never mind, Roger. I'll go down myself."

"Aren't you afraid?"

"Not now. I wouldn't have been of this Stumpy only he came on me so suddenly. I'll go at once."

"You'd better," said a voice behind her. "Your five minutes is up, Miss Kate." And Booth appeared at the head of the stairs and motioned her down.

"Good-by, Roger. I'm so sorry to leave you here alone."

"It's not such a dreadful place," I rejoined lightly. "If you discover anything, let me know at once."

"Be sure I will." And with this assurance Kate was gone.

I was as sorry for her as I was for myself. I knew all she would have to face in public—the mean things people would say to her, the snubbing she would be called on to bear.

The loss of the statement rendered me doubly downhearted. Oh, how much I had counted on it, assuring myself over and over again that it would surely clear my father's name!

Hardly had my sister left me than there were more voices below, and I heard Mr. Woodward tell Booth that he had an order from Judge Penfold for a private interview with me.

"Better go right upstairs then, Mr. Woodward," was the jailer's reply. "He's all alone."

I wondered what the merchant's visit could portend, but had

Edward Stratemeyer

little time for speculation.

"So, sir, they've got you fast," said Mr. Woodward sharply as he faced me. "Fast, and no mistake."

"What do you want?" I demanded boldly, coming at once to the front.

"What do I want?" repeated the merchant, looking behind him to make sure that Booth had not followed him. "What do I want? Why, I want to help you, Strong, that's what I want."

I could not help but smile. The idea of Mr. Woodward helping any one, least of all myself!

"The only way you can help me is to set me free," I returned.

"Oh, I can't do that. You are held on the Canby charge solely."

"But you told me you wanted me arrested."

"So I did, but I intend to give you a chance—that is, if you will do what I want."

"But why did you want me arrested?"

"You know well enough, Strong."

"On the contrary, I haven't the least idea."

"Stuff and nonsense. See here, if you want to get off without further trouble, hand over those papers."

"What papers?"

"The papers you took last night," replied Mr. Woodward, sharply.

I was truly astonished. How in the world had he found out about the statement dropped by Stumpy? Was it possible there had been a meeting between the two? It looked like it.

"I haven't got the papers," I rejoined.

"Don't tell me a falsehood sir," he thundered.

"It's true."

"Do you deny you have the packet?"

"I do."

"Come, Strong, that story won't answer. Hand it over."

"I haven't it."

"Where is it?"

"I lost it," I replied, before I had time to think.

"Lost it!" he cried anxiously.

"Yes, sir," I returned boldly, resolved to make the best of it, now the cat was out of the bag. "Either that or it was stolen from me."

He looked at me in silence for a moment.

"Do you expect me to believe all your lies?" he demanded finally.

"I don't care what you believe," I answered. "I tell the truth. And one question I want to ask you, Aaron Woodward. Why are you so anxious to gain possession of Nicholas Weaver's dying statement?"

The merchant gave a cry of astonishment, nay, horror. He turned pale and glared at me fiercely.

"Nicholas Weaver's dying statement!" he ejaculated. "What do you know of Nicholas Weaver?"

Now I had spoken I was almost sorry I had said what I had. Yet I could not but notice the tremendous effect my words had produced.

"Never mind what I know," I replied. "Why do you take an interest in it?"

"I? I don't know anything about it," he faltered. "I hardly knew Nicholas Weaver."

"Indeed? Yet you want his statement."

"No, I don't. I don't know anything about his statement," he continued doggedly. "I want my papers. I don't care a rap about any one else's."

It was now my turn to be astonished. Evidently I had been on the wrong track from the beginning.

"If you don't want his statement, I'm sure I don't know what you do want," I rejoined, and I spoke the exact truth.

"Don't tell lies, Strong. You know well enough. Hand them over."

"Hand what over?"

"The packet of papers."

"I haven't any packet."

"Strong, if you don't do as I demand, I'll send you to prison after your father."

"I can't help it. I haven't any papers. If you don't believe me, search me."

"Where have you hidden them?"

"I never had them to hide."

"I know better, sir, I know better," he fumed.

I made no reply. What could I say?

"Do you hear me, Strong?"

For reply I walked over to the slatted window and began to whistle. My action only increased the merchant's anger.

"For the last time, Strong, will you give up the papers?" he cried.

"For the last time, Mr. Woodward, let me say I haven't got them, never had them, and, therefore, cannot possibly give them up."

"Then you shall go to prison, sir. Mark my word,—you shall go to prison!"

And with this parting threat the merchant hurried down the

loft steps and rapped loudly for Booth to come and let him out.

When he was gone, I sat down again to think over the demand he had made upon me. To what papers did he refer? In vain I cudgelled my brain to elicit an answer.

He spoke about sending me to prison, and in such tones as if it were an easy matter to do. Assuredly he must have some grounds upon which to base so positive an assertion.

No doubt he was now on his way to Judge Penfold's office to swear out the necessary papers. I did not know much about the law, but I objected strongly to going to prison. Once in a regular lockup, the chances of getting out would be indeed slim.

I reasoned that the best thing to do was to escape while there was a chance. Perhaps I was wrong in this conclusion, but I was only a country boy, and I had a horror of stone walls and iron bars.

Escape! No sooner had the thought entered my mind than I was wrapped up in it. Undoubtedly it was the best thing to do. Freedom meant not only liberty, but also a chance to hunt down John Stumpy and clear my father's name.

I looked about the loft for the best means of accomplishing my purpose. As I have said, the place was over a carpenter shop. The roof was sloping to the floor, and at each end was a small window heavily slatted.

The distance to the ground from the window was not less than fifteen feet, rather a long drop even if I could manage to get the slats loose, which I doubted, for I had no tools at hand.

I resolved to try the door, and was about to do so when I heard the bolts shoot back and Booth appeared.

For an instant I thought to trip him up and rush past him, but he stood on the steps completely blocking the way.

"All right, Roger?" he asked.

"Yes, sir."

"Quite com'table, boy?"

"As comfortable as any one could be in such a place," I rejoined lightly.

"'Tain't exactly a parlor," he chuckled. "No easy chairs or sofys; but the food's good. I'm a-going to get it for you now. Then after that maybe the judge will call around. I'll bring the dinner in a minute."

He climbed downstairs, bolting the door after him.

In five minutes—or ten at the most—I knew he would be back. After that there was no telling how long he would stay.

Now, therefore, was the proper time to escape, now or never!

# CHAPTER XII

## A SURPRISE

No time must be lost. Booth lived but a short hundred feet from the jail, if such it might be called, and if his wife had dinner ready it would not take him long to bring it.

I surveyed the room in which I was incarcerated critically. Escape by either window was, as I have intimated, out of the question. On account of its height, the scuttle was also not to be considered.

Apparently nothing remained to try but the door. Running down the steps, I looked it over. It was of solid oak planking, an inch thick, and fastened at both top and bottom.

It was a hard thing to tackle, especially with no tools, and, after surveying it, I went upstairs again to search for something that might do as a pry.

I could see nothing but the empty nail keg, and I could discover no use at first in this until the idea struck me of wedging it between one of the lower steps and the door, and, by jumping upon it, forcing the bottom bolt.

With some difficulty I placed the keg in position and brought down my full weight upon it. The first time the bolt merely creaked, but the second there was a snap, and the lower part of the door burst outward several inches.

The bottom bolt had yielded, and now only the top one remained. But to reach this was a difficult matter, as no purchase could be had against it.

While considering the situation, I imagined I heard my jailer returning, and my heart jumped into my throat. What if Booth should see the damage I had done? I reckoned that things would go hard with me if it became known that I had attempted to break jail. Judge Penfold would surely give me the full penalty of the law.

But the approach of Booth was only imaginary, and, after a brief interval of silence, I breathed freer.

I ascends the stairs once more to see if I could not find something besides the keg to assist me. If only I had a plank or a beam, I might use it as a battering-ram.

The thought of a plank led me to examine the floor, and, going over it carefully, I soon came to a short board, one end of which was loose. Raising it, I pulled with all my might, and the board came up.

I was astonished to see that it made an opening into the shop below. I had imagined that the floor or ceiling was of double thickness.

This gave me a new idea. Why not escape through the floor? To pry up another board would perhaps be easier than to force the door.

I tried the board next to the opening. The end was somewhat

rotted, and it came up with hardly an effort.

In another moment the opening would be large enough to allow the passage of my body. Putting the first board under the edge of the second, I bore down upon it.

As I did so I heard a noise that alarmed me greatly. It was the sound of Booth returning, and the next instant the carpenter had opened the outer door and entered.

In one hand he carried a tray containing my dinner. He crossed the floor directly under me without looking up. Then his eyes caught the shattered door and he gave a loud exclamation.

"By ginger! If that boy ain't gone and escaped!"

He set down the tray with a rattle and tried to pull the door open. But the top bolt had become displaced, and it was several seconds before it could be shot back.

Meanwhile I was not idle. As quietly as I could I tore up the second board. The deed was done just as Booth stumbled over the keg on his way up the stairs.

As my jailer appeared at the top, I let my body through the opening. It was a tight squeeze, especially when accomplished in a hurry. I landed in a heap on a pile of shavings.

"Stop! stop!" called out Booth. "Roger, don't you hear me?"

I certainly did hear him, but paid no attention to his words. My one thought was to get away as quickly as possible.

"If you don't stop, I'll shoot you," went on Booth at the top of his voice. "Don't you know breaking jail is a—a felony?"

I did not know what kind of a crime it was. I had made up my mind to escape, and intended to do so, even if such a deed constituted manslaughter. I made a break for the door and passed out just as Booth came tramping down the stairs.

I ran across the yard that separated the carpenter shop from the house. As I did so, Mrs. Booth appeared at the back door. Upon seeing me she held up her hands in horror.

"Mercy on us! Roger Strong! Where be you a-running to? 'Zekel! 'Zekel! the prisoner's broke loose!"

"I know it, Mandy!" I heard Ezekiel Booth answer. "Dunno how he did it, though. Stop, Roger, it's best now; jest you mark my word!"

I heard no more. Jumping the side fence, I ran through a bit of orchard and across a stony lot until I reached the Pass River.

At this point this body of water was several hundred feet wide. The bank sloped directly to the water's edge. Near at hand were several private boat-houses, one belonging to Mr. Aaron Woodward, he having built it to please Duncan.

At the end of the boat-house pier lay a skiff, the oars resting upon the seats. I knew it was wrong to make use of the craft, but "necessity knows no law," and my need was great.

Running down to the end of the pier, I dropped into the boat and shoved off. As I did so, Duncan Woodward, accompanied by Pultzer, came out of the boat-house.

"Hi, there, what are you doing in my boat?" he sang out. "What, Roger Strong!" he continued as he came nearer.

Edward Stratemeyer

"You must lend me the boat, Duncan," I returned. "I've got to cross the river in a hurry."

"Not much! I thought you were in jail."

"Not just now," I replied. "You can get your boat on the other side."

"Hold up! You shan't have her. Come back!"

But I was already pulling out into the stream. He continued to shout after me, and presently I saw the two joined by Booth, and all watched me in dismay as I made for the opposite shore.

Reaching the bank, I beached the boat high up and then climbed to the roadway that ran beside the stream. Trees and bushes were thick here, and I had but little difficulty in hiding from the view of those opposite.

For a moment I hesitated as to which way to proceed. A number of miles down the stream lay Newville, of which I have already spoken. Probably my pursuers would think I had gone in that direction. If so, they would hasten to the bridge below, with the intention of cutting me off.

I therefore started immediately on my way up the river road, resolved to put as much ground as possible between myself and my pursuers. I had no definite destination in view, but thought to gain some hiding-place where I might rest secure and think things over.

It was now going on to two o'clock in the afternoon, and as I had not had anything to eat since the noon previous, I began to feel decidedly hungry. I felt in my pocket and discovered that I was the possessor of sixty-five cents, and with this amount of cash I did not see any reason for my remaining hungry any longer.

Presently I came to a small, white cottage, upon the front porch of which was displayed the sign

BOARDING

Ascending the steps, I knocked at the door, and a comely, middle-aged woman answered my summons.

"I see that you take boarders here," I said, "I am hungry, and several miles from any restaurant. Can you furnish me with dinner?"

She looked me over rather sharply before replying. Then I realize for the first time that my appearance was not of the best. My clothes were considerably the worse for having rolled over and over in the old tool house, and in escaping from my prison I had made several rents in my coat.

"I will pay you whatever you charge," I added hastily, "and I would like to wash and brush up, too; I have had a tumble," which was literally true.

"I can let you have dinner for twenty-five cent," she said finally. "I won't charge you anything for cleaning up," she added, with something like a smile. "Will you mind paying in advance?"

"No, ma'am," and I handed over the money. "I suppose I won't have to wait very long."

"Oh, no, the regular boarders have just finished. You can sit right down."

"If you don't mind, I'll take a wash first."

The woman led the way to an ante-room, in which were placed a bowl of water, towel, and soap, as well as a dust brush. It did not take me long to fix myself up, and then I flattered myself I did not present an unbecoming appearance.

The dinner that the woman served was not as good as that which my sister Kate helped to prepare at the Widow Canby's, but it was wholesome food, and my sharpened appetite made it disappear rapidly.

As I ate I reflected upon my situation. For the life of me I did not know what to do next. I longed to see my sister and tell her that I was safe. This done, I intended to devote my time to hunting up the man who I firmly believed held my father's reputation in his hand. I was sure I would discover him sooner or later, and this accomplished, I would not let him out of my sight until he had confessed his secret. I wondered if Kate had succeeded in finding that precious statement I had lost. Heartily did I reproach myself for not having taken better care of it.

Having satisfied myself upon the substantial things set before me, I finished my meal with a small cut of apple pie.

As I was swallowing the last mouthful I glanced out of the window up the road, and gave a cry of surprise. And no wonder, for coming toward the house was Mr. Aaron Woodward, and beside him walked John Stumpy!

# CHAPTER XIII

## AN INTERESTING CONVERSATION

I could hardly believe the evidence of my senses when I saw Mr. Aaron Woodward coming up the road with John Stumpy beside him. It would have astonished me to have seen the merchant alone, but to see him in company with the very man I was looking for was more than I had thought possible.

Yet I reflected that the tramp—or whatever the man was—had evinced a determination to secure an interview with Mr. Woodward before quitting Darbyville. There was important business to be transacted between them. Mr. John Stumpy intended to have his say, whatever that might mean.

What was to be done? It would never do for me to be seen. Nothing short of arrest would follow. I must get out of the way as quickly as possible.

During the time I had been eating, the sky had become overcast as if a shower was imminent. Taking advantage of this fact I rose quickly and reached for my hat.

"Guess we're going to have a thunder shower," I remarked. "Hope it holds off. I don't want to get wet."

"Then you'll have to hurry," rejoined the woman as she looked out of the door. "Looks as if it would be here in less than quarter of an hour."

"Then I'm off. Good day."

"Good day. Come again."

I slipped out of the door, and passing behind a hedge, made my way to the road. As I did so, Mr. Woodward and Stumpy turned from the highway and walked directly up the gravel path that led to the house!

I was dumfounded by this movement. What did they mean by going to the very place I had just vacated? Was it possible they had seen me?

I earnestly hoped not; for if so, it would spoil a little plan that had just come to me, which was to follow them, see what they were up to, and, if possible, overhear whatever might be said.

I was soon convinced that neither of the men was aware of my presence. They were talking earnestly and stepped up on the porch just as ordinary visitors would have done. In a moment the woman let them in and the door closed behind them.

My curiosity was aroused to its highest pitch, and at the risk of being discovered by any one who might chance to be passing by I walked cautiously back along the hedge until I reached a clump of rose bushes that grew directly under one of the dining-room windows.

The window was open, and by a little manoeuvring I easily managed to see and hear what was going on within.

"You came for the rent, I suppose, Mr. Woodward," the woman was saying. "Joel was going to bring it up to-night. He would have brought it over this morning, only he thought it was going to rain and he had some hay he wanted to get in."

"Yes, I did come for the rent, Mrs. Decker," replied the merchant. "It's due several days now."

"I have it here—thirty dollars. Here is the receipt book."

There was the rustle of bills and the scratching of a pen.

"Here you are, Mrs. Decker."

"Thank you, sir. Now we'll be worry free for another month."

"So you are. Nothing like being prompt."

"My husband was going to speak to you about the roof. It leaks dreadfully."

"Pooh! That can't be. Why, it was patched only two years ago."

"You are wrong, Mr. Woodward. It is four years, and then but very little was done to it."

"It cost near twelve dollars," growled the merchant. "You can't expect me to be fixing up the house all the time."

"It leaks very badly."

"Then your husband will have to attend to it. I can't spend any more money this year."

Edward Stratemeyer

"I don't know what we'll do. I wish you would just step outside and look up at the shingles. Nearly all of them are ready to fall off."

I was alarmed by Mrs. Decker's request. Suppose the trio should come out? I would surely be discovered. But my fears were groundless, as the next words of Mr. Woodward proved.

"I can't go out now, madam, not now. I haven't time. I have a little business to transact with this man, and then I must return to Darbyville."

"I'm sorry—" began the woman.

"So am I; but it cannot be helped. Can I use this room for a while?"

By the look upon Mrs. Decker's face it was plain to see she wanted to say, "No, you can't," but she hardly dared to speak the words, so she gave an icy assent and withdrew.

The merchant followed her to the door and saw that it was closed tightly behind her. Then he strode across the room and faced John Stumpy.

"Wall, sir, now we'll have an accounting," he began in an authoritative voice.

"So we will, Woody," returned John Stumpy, in no wise abashed by the other's manner.

The merchant winced at the use of a nickname, but after an instant's hesitation passed it over.

"What do you mean by coming to Darbyville, sir, when I

have repeatedly written you to stay away?"

"Oh, come, Woody, don't get on your high horse," was Stumpy's response, as he swung back in the rocker he occupied. "You know I never could stand your high-toned ways."

"I flatter myself I am a trifle above common people," returned Mr. Woodward, and it was plain to see where Duncan got his arrogant manner.

"Oh, pshaw! don't make me tired," yawned Stumpy. "Come, let's to business."

"I am at business. Why did you come here?"

"You know well enough. Didn't I write to you?"

"Yes, and got my answer. We've squared up accounts, sir."

"Don't 'sir' me,—it don't go down," cried Stumpy, angrily. "We haven't squared up, not by a jugful,—not till you hand over some more cash."

"I've handed over enough now."

"No, you hain't. Do you think I'm going to do all your work for nothing?"

"You were well paid."

"It's only you as thinks so; I don't."

"How much more do you want?"

"A thousand dollars."

Edward Stratemeyer

The largeness of the demand fairly took away my breath. As for Mr. Aaron Woodward, he was beside himself.

"A thousand dollars!" he said. "Why, you're crazy, sir."

"No, I ain't; I mean just what I say."

"You expect me to pay you a thousand dollars?"

"Of course I do. I wouldn't ask it if I didn't."

"See here, Fer—"

"Sh!—John Stumpy, if you please."

"That's so, I forgot. But see here, a thousand dollars! Why, I've already paid you that."

"So you have. Now I want another thousand and then we'll cry quits."

Mr. Aaron Woodward grew white with rage. "I never heard of such an outrageous demand," he cried. "I'll never pay it."

"Oh, yes, you will," rejoined the other, coolly. "Aaron Woodward never yet acted rashly."

"Suppose I refuse to pay?"

"Better not; I'm a bad man when I am aroused."

"I don't fear you. You can do nothing to me."

"Oh, yes, I can. I can tell ugly stories about Mr. Aaron Woodward; stories concerning his doings when he was collector for Holland & Mack."

"And who would believe you?" sneered the merchant. "You, a common tramp—"

"Tramp, am I—" interrupted John Stumpy, with a scowl. "If I am, who made me so?"

"Your own self and the bottle. Do you think you can hurt me? Nonsense!"

"I can try."

"And who will believe you, I repeat? A common tramp— whom the police are now hunting for, because of a robbery that occurred only last night."

" 'Tain't so!"

"It is. You broke into the Widow Canby's house and stole over two hundred dollars."

In spite of the dirt on his face, John Stumpy grew pale.

"Who can prove it?"

"Several people. Carson Strong's son, for one."

Stumpy sprang to his feet. Then almost as suddenly sat down.

"Didn't know he had a son," he said, as carelessly as he could.

"Yes, you did," returned the merchant, flatly. "I think, Fer— Stumpy, I know a little more about you than you do about me."

Bitter hatred spread itself over the tramp's face.

"Oh, ho, you do, do you? Well, we'll see. 'Them laughs best as laughs last.' If you won't pay, I'm off."

He rose to his feet and reached for his hat, Mr. Woodward intercepted him.

"Where are you going?"

"That's my business. I want you to know I didn't come on all the way from Chicago for nothing."

"Are you hard up?"

"Yes, I am. I want money, and I'm going to have it."

"How about the two hundred dollars you stole last night?"

Stumpy hesitated.

"Well, if you want to know the truth, I lost the money," he said.

# CHAPTER XIV

## THE PRICE OF SILENCE

For a moment I was staggered by John Stumpy's announcement. Was it possible he was telling the truth? If so, the chances of recovering the Widow Canby's money would assume a different shape. To arrest him would prove a moral satisfaction, but it would not restore the stolen dollars.

Occupying the position I did, I was more interested in restoring the stolen money than I was in having the tramp incarcerated.

Nothing would have given me greater satisfaction than to have met the Widow Canby at the depot with the two hundred odd dollars in my pocket. It would have silenced the public tongue and made my breaking jail of no consequence.

But perhaps John Stumpy was telling a falsehood. He was not above such a thing, and would not hesitate if he thought anything could be gained thereby. That Mr. Aaron Woodward also guessed such to be a fact was proven by the words that followed Stumpy's statement.

"Lost the money?" he ejaculated. "Do you expect me to believe you, sir?"

Edward Stratemeyer

"It's true."

"Nonsense, sir. Jack Fer—"

"Sh!"

"John Stumpy isn't the one to lose over two hundred dollars!"

"Just what I always said myself, partner, and—"

"Don't 'partner ' me, sir!"

"Well, wasn't we all partners in the good times gone by?"

"No, sir!"

"I reckon we were. Howsomever, let it pass. Well, as I was saying, I reckoned I'd never lose any money, leasewise a small pile, but that's what I have done, and that's why I want you to come down."

And John Stumpy leaned back in the rocker in a defiant fashion.

The merchant eyed him sharply in silence for a moment.

"Where did you lose the money?" he asked at length.

"How do I know? If I did, don't you suppose I'd go back and pick it up?"

"I thought perhaps you were afraid of discovery."

"Humph! I'm not skeered of any such constables as they have in Darbyville."

"But you must have some idea where you dropped it," went on Mr. Woodward, and I was astonished to see how coolly this man, who always pretended to be so straightforward, could inquire about stolen money.

"Not the least," responded John Stumpy. "There was two hundred and sixty dollars in all. I took out ten and left the rest in the pocketbook it was in. I've got the ten dollars, and that's all. And that's why you've got to come down," he went on deliberately. "I'm off for Chicago to-night, and I'm not going back empty handed."

"You think I ought to pay you for your own carelessness," returned Mr. Woodward, coolly.

"Not a bit of it. You owe me every cent I ask."

"I don't owe you a penny."

"You owe me a thousand dollars, and for the last time let me tell you, you've got to pay or take the consequences." And John Stumpy brought his fist down on the table with a bang.

"Hold on; don't make so much noise," cried Mr. Aaron Woodward in alarm. "There is no use of rousing the household."

"I don't care. Either you'll come down or I'll rouse the whole of Darbyville," cried the tramp, vehemently.

"I haven't any money."

"You can't tell me that."

"It's true. Times are getting worse every day."

Edward Stratemeyer

"Didn't the woman who lives here just pay you?"

"Yes; thirty dollars—"

"And didn't you put the bills in with a big roll in your vest pocket?" went on Stumpy, triumphantly.

The merchant bit his lip.

"That money is to pay a bill that falls due to-morrow," he replied.

"Well, my 'bill' falls due to-day, and it's got to be met. So come; no more beating about the bush. We've talked long enough. Now to business. Do you intend to pay or not?"

The merchant hesitated. Evidently he was afraid to oppose the other too strongly.

"Well, I don't want to let you go without anything," he began. "I'll let you have twenty-five dollars—"

John Stumpy jumped up in a passion. "That settles it. I'm done with you. To-night I'll send a letter to Chris Holtzmann, 897 Sherman Street, Chicago, and tell him a few things he wants to know, and—"

"You dare!" almost shrieked Mr. Woodward. "Write a single word to him and I'll—I'll—"

"So! ho! You're afraid of him, are you?"

"No, I'm not, but what's the use of letting him know anything?"

"Humph! Do you suppose I'd tell him without pay? Not

much! I can easily get him to fork over fifty or a hundred dollars. And he'll make you pay it back, ten times over."

Mr. Aaron Woodward sank back in a chair without a word. Evidently he was completely baffled, and knew not which way to turn.

As for myself, I was very much in the dark as to what all this was about. I was certain the past events spoken of pertained to my father's affairs, but failed to "make connections."

One thing, however, I did do, and that was to make a note of Mr. Chris Holtzmann's address. He was the man Stumpy had written to just previous to the robbery, and he was perhaps one of the persons concerned in my father's downfall.

"See here," said the merchant at last. "It's too late for us to quarrel. What good would an exposure to Holtzmann do?"

"Never mind. If you won't come to time, I shall do as I please," growled Stumpy.

"But a thousand dollars! I haven't got it in cash."

"You can easily get it."

"Not so easily as you think. Tell you what I will do. I'll give you a hundred. But you must give up all evidence you have against me."

Stumpy gave a short, contemptuous laugh. "You must think me as green as grass," he sneered. "I'm not giving up any evidence. I'm holding on to all I've got and gathering more."

"You have Nicholas Weaver's statement," went on Mr. Woodward, with interest.

"So I have. Nick told the truth in it, too."

"I would like to see it"

"Of course you would. So would some other people,— Carson Strong's boy, for instance."

"Sh!—not so loud."

"Well, then, don't bring the subject up."

"Have you the statement with you?"

"Maybe I haven't; maybe I have."

"Perhaps it was taken from you," went on Mr. Woodward, curiously.

"What do you know about that?" Stumpy again jumped to his feet. "You've been talking to that Strong boy," he cried.

"Supposing I have?"

"Well, it didn't do you no good. Say, how much does the young cub know?"

"He knows too much for the good of either of us," responded the merchant.

"Sorry he wasn't found in the ruins of that tool house," growled the tramp, savagely.

This was certainly a fine assertion for me to hear. Yet it was no more than I would expect from John Stumpy. He was a villain through and through.

"You meant to burn him up, did you?" asked Mr. Woodward.

"And if I had, Mr. Aaron Woodward would never have shed a tear," laughed John Stumpy.

"Let me see the statement."

John Stumpy hesitated. "Hand over the money first, and maybe I will."

"The hundred dollars?"

"No, a thousand."

"Do you suppose I carry so much money with me?"

"Give me what you have in that roll, and I'll take your word for the rest."

The merchant gave something that sounded very much like a groan.

"Well, I suppose if you insist on it, I must," he said. "I'll give you what I have, but I won't promise you any more."

"Hand it over," was Stumpy's laconic reply. He probably thought half a loaf better than no bread, at all.

With a heavy sigh Mr. Woodward drew the roll of bills from his pocket and began to count them over. I was eager to catch sight of them. I stood on tiptoe and peered into the window. It was an interesting scene; the sour look upon the merchant's face; the look of greed in the tramp's eye. In a moment the counting was finished.

Edward Stratemeyer

"A hundred and seventy dollars," said Mr. Aaron Woodward. "Here you are." And he held them out. Stumpy almost snatched them from his hand.

"There, now that's settled," he said. "Now about—What was that?"

A noise had disturbed him. While absorbed in what the two were doing I had given an involuntary cough.

"Somebody listening," he declared as he thrust the money into his pocket.

"We ought to be more careful."

"Only some one coughing in the next room," returned Mr. Woodward. "Don't get scared."

"I ain't scared, but I don't want other folks to know my business. Reckon you don't either."

"No, indeed. It's bad enough for me to be seen in your company," returned Mr. Aaron Woodward, with just a trace of his former lofty manner.

"No insinuations, please," was the ready reply. "My hands ain't any dirtier than yours."

"Well, well, let's stop quarrelling. Let me see the statement."

"Will you promise to hand it back if I do?"

"Why not let me have it?"

"Never mind why. Will you give it back?"

"If you insist on it, you shall have it back," was Mr. Woodward's final reply, seeing that he could gain nothing by parleying.

Stumpy drew forth the envelope. I anticipated what was coming.

"Here it is," he said, and handed it over, as he supposed.

"The envelope is empty," said Mr. Woodward.

Stumpy looked dumfounded.

# CHAPTER XV

## AN ODD STATEMENT

Before Mr. Woodward made the announcement just recorded he had walked close up to the window, probably to get into the light, for the sky was now darkening rapidly, portending the near breaking out of the storm I have mentioned.

In doing this the merchant's back was turned upon his companion, and for an instant Stumpy had been unable to see what the other was doing.

When therefore Mr. Woodward declared the envelope to be empty every action of the tramp indicated that he did not believe the statement.

"Empty?" he cried hoarsely.

"Yes, empty," replied the merchant; "and you knew it," he added.

"No such thing. The statement was inside. Woody, you're trying to play a sharp game, but it won't work."

"What do you mean, sir?"

"You're trying to rob me."

"Nonsense. I say the envelope was empty."

"And I say it wasn't. Come, hand over my property."

"I tell you, Fer—Stumpy, I haven't it."

"I don't care what you say. You can't play any such game off on me," rejoined John Stumpy, with increasing anger.

"I'm only speaking the truth."

"You ain't. Hand it over, or I'll—"

John Stumpy caught the merchant by the coat collar.

"What would you do?" cried Mr. Woodward in alarm, and it was plain to see he was a coward at heart.

"I'll choke the life out of you; that's what I'll do. Hand over the statement."

"I haven't it, upon my honor."

"Your honor? Bah! What does that amount to?"

John Stumpy suddenly shifted his hand from its grasp on the collar to the merchant's throat. For a moment I thought Mr. Woodward was in danger of being choked to death.

"Stop! Stop! Se—search me if you—you want to," he gasped.

But John Stumpy's passion seemed to have got the better of his reason. He did not relax his hold in the least.

Edward Stratemeyer

A short struggle ensued. The two backed up against the table, and presently a chair was upset. Of course all this made considerable noise. Yet neither of the men heeded it.

Presently the door from the other room swung open, and the two had hardly time to separate before a tall, lank farmer entered.

"Hello, what's up?" he asked in a loud, drawling tone.

For an instant neither spoke, evidently not knowing what to say.

"We were—were—ahem—trying to—to catch a rat," replied Mr. Woodward, with an effort.

"A rat?"

"Exactly, sir. Had a terrible time with him, Mr. Decker."

The farmer looked surprised. "So I supposed by the row that was going on," he said. "Curious. I knew there were rats down to the barn, but I didn't suppose they came up to the house. What became of him?"

"Slipped out of the door just now," put in John Stumpy. "There he goes!" he added, pointing out into the hall.

Mr. Decker made a spring out of the room.

"I must ketch him, by gopher!" he cried. "There's enough eat up here now without having the vermin taking a hand in."

Mr. Woodward closed the door after the man.

"Now see to what your actions have brought us," he

exclaimed. "If it hadn't been for my quick wit we'd been in a pretty mess."

"Not my fault," growled John Stumpy. "Why don't you give up the statement?"

I could not help but feel amused at his persistency. His demands upon the merchant were about on a footing with those Mr. Woodward had made upon me.

"If you'll only listen to reason," began the merchant, "I will prove—"

The rest of his remark was drowned out in a clap of thunder. Somewhat startled, I looked up at the sky.

The black clouds in the south had rolled up rapidly, until now the entire horizon was covered. The first burst of thunder was succeeded directly by several others, and then large drops of rain began to fall.

The wind blew the drops directly into the window. I crouched down out of sight, and the next moment Mr. Woodward said:—

"It's raining in the window. We'd better close it up."

Of course directly the window was closed I could hear no longer. I remained in my position for half a minute or more, and then as the rain began to pour down rapidly I made a break for better shelter.

I sought the barn. It was a low, rambling structure, with great wide doors. No one seemed to be around, and I rushed in without ceremony. I was pretty fairly soaked, but as it was warm I did not mind the ducking. I shook out my hat and coat and then sat down to think matters over.

What I had heard had not given me much satisfaction. To be sure, it had proved beyond a doubt that Mr. Aaron Woodward was a thorough scoundrel, but of this I had been already satisfied in my own mind.

What was I to do? I had asked myself that question several times, and now I asked it again.

If only I could get John Stumpy arrested, perhaps it would be possible to force him to make a confession. But how was this to be done?

While I sat on the edge of a feed box, a form darkened the doorway, and Farmer Decker appeared.

"Hello!" he exclaimed. "What are you doing here?"

"I took the liberty to come in out of the rain," I replied. "Have you any objections to my remaining until the shower is over?"

"No, guess not. It's a mighty heavy one. Where're you from? Newville?"

"No, sir, Darbyville."

"Yes? Had quite a robbery down there, I understand."

"Is that so?"

"Yes, a chap named Strong robbed an old woman of nearly five hundred dollars. Do you know him or the woman?"

"I know the woman quite well," was my reply, and I hoped

he would not question me further.

"They've got him in jail, I believe. The fellow and his sister tried to make out that a tramp had taken the money, but I understand no one would listen to the story."

"No?"

"No. It seems this Strong boy's father is in jail now for stealing, so it ain't strange the boy's a thief."

"But maybe he isn't guilty," I put in, by way of a mild protest.

"Maybe. Of course it's rather tough on him if he isn't. But you can't tell nowadays; boys is so all-fired high toned, and want to play big fiddle."

"Some boys are, but not all of them."

"Some of them. Now there's our landlord, who is in the house now, he's got a son as extravagant as can be, and if it wasn't for Mr. Woodward keeping him in funds I don't know what that boy might not do. He—whoa, there, Billy, whoa!"

The last remark was addressed to a horse standing in one of the stalls. A clap of thunder had set the animal to prancing.

"Your horse feels rather uneasy," I remarked, glad of a chance to change the subject.

"Allers acts that way when there's a storm going on. Too bad, too, for I want to hitch him up and take Mr. Woodward and another man that's with him over to Darbyville."

As Mr. Decker spoke he led the horse from the stall and

backed him up between the shafts of the carriage that stood near the rear of the barn.

While he was hitching up I set myself to thinking. While I was perfectly willing that Mr. Woodward should return to Darbyville, I did not wish to allow John Stumpy out of my sight. Once away, and I might not be able to lay hands on him.

Had I been sure that Kate had succeeded in finding the lost statement, I would not have cared, but the chances in her favor were slim, and I did not wish to run any risks.

"Are you going to drive around to the house for them?" I asked as the farmer finished the job.

"Guess I'll have to. It will be a beastly drive. Sorry I can't offer you a seat—it would be better than walking."

"I think I'll wait till it clears off," I returned. "I'm not on business, and—"

"Say, Decker, how long is it going to take you to hitch up?" interrupted a voice from the doorway, and the next instant Mr. Woodward strode into the barn, followed by John Stumpy.

I did not have time to conceal myself. I tried to step behind a partition, but before I could do so the merchant's eye was on me.

"Roger Strong!" he exclaimed.

"Yes, sir," I replied, as boldly as I could.

"How did you get here?" he demanded.

"Walked, just as you did."

"Thought you were in jail."

"So do most people."

"Who is this chap?" asked the farmer, staring at me with open eyes.

"It's the boy who was arrested for that robbery last night," explained the merchant.

"Shoo—you don't say? And I was talking to him about that very thing. You rascal, you!"

"How did you get out?" put in John Stumpy.

"None of your business," I replied briskly. "If you'd had your way I'd been burnt up in the tool house last night."

"No such thing," was the tramp's reply. "Never saw you before."

"You're the fellow who stole the Widow Canby's money."

"You must be crazy, young fellow. I don't know anything about the Widow Canby or her money."

"I can prove it. My sister can prove it, too."

"Then your sister must be as crazy as yourself."

"Stop there! You're the thief and you know it."

"I know nothing of the kind."

"Your story is nonsensical, Strong," broke in Mr. Woodward. "Gentlemen like Mr. Stumpy here do not break into people's houses and commit robberies."

"Gentlemen! He's nothing but a tramp, and you know it."

"Tramp? How dare you?" cried Stumpy, in suddenly assumed dignity, put on for the farmer's benefit. "I am a ranchero from Texas and an honest man. I am visiting Mr. Woodward, and know nothing more of the robbery excepting having heard that it occurred—ahem!" And John Stumpy drew himself up.

Under other circumstances I would have laughed at his effrontery. But the situation was too serious to indulge in any humor.

"Being placed under arrest has turned your head, Strong," said the merchant. "You seem to be quite out of your mind."

"When was the robbery committed?" put in John Stumpy, suddenly.

"You know well enough," I cried.

"I heard it was about two o'clock in the morning," vouchsafed Farmer Decker.

"Then I can easily prove an alibi," said the tramp, triumphantly. "I can prove I was with my esteemed friend Mr. Woodward at that hour. Isn't it so, Aaron?"

The merchant hesitated. I fairly held my breath to catch his answer. Would he commit deliberate perjury?

"Quite true," he replied slowly. "Mr. Stumpy was with me

last night. We sat up in the library, smoking, and playing cards until after midnight, and then I showed him to bed. He could not possibly have committed the crime of which Strong speaks."

"Then the boy must be the guilty one hisself," said the farmer. "And so young, too. Who would a-thought it! What shall we do with him, Mr. Woodward?"

"You had better help me take him back to Darbyville jail," responded the merchant.

## CHAPTER XVI

## MY UNCLE ENOS

John Stumpy gave a smile of triumph. As for myself, I stood aghast. Mr. Aaron Woodward had committed deliberate perjury, or at least, something that amounted to the same thing. He had positively declared that John Stumpy was at his house at the time of the robbery of Widow Canby's house, and could not, therefore, be the guilty party.

It was easy to guess that in this statement it was his intention to screen his partner in iniquity. To be sure, he had been forced to take the position by Stumpy himself, but once having taken it, I was morally certain he would not back down.

His action would make it harder than ever for me to clear myself and bring the tramp to justice. His word in a court of law would carry more weight than mine or my sister's, and consequently our case would fall to the ground.

I was glad that Dick Blair could testify concerning my whereabouts and the scene in the dining room directly after the robbery. The merchant knew nothing of Blair's presence on the occasion—at least I imagined so from his conversation—and might, by saying too much, "put his foot in it."

But now my mind was filled with only one thought. The three men intended to take me to the Darbyville jail. I was to be ignominiously dragged back to the prison from which I had escaped.

Once again in Ezekiel Booth's custody I was certain he would keep so strict a guard over me that further breaking away would be out of the question. Perhaps Judge Penfold would consider me so dangerous a prisoner as to send me to the county jail for safe keeping, in which case it would be harder than ever for me to clear myself or see Kate.

For an instant I meditated taking to my legs and running my chances, but this idea was knocked in the head by Farmer Decker grasping me by the collar.

"Maybe he might take a notion and run away," he explained. "He did it once, you say."

"A good idea to hold him," said Mr. Woodward. "Have you finished hitching up?"

"Yes, sir."

"Have you room for him?"

"I might put in another seat."

"Do so. And hurry; the rain has slackened up a bit, and we may reach Darbyville before it starts again."

The extra seat was soon placed in the carriage. Then the farmer procured a couple of rubber blankets.

"All ready now," he said. "How shall we sit?"

Edward Stratemeyer

"You and Mr. Stumpy sit in front. I and the boy will occupy the back seat. Come, Strong, get in."

For an instant I thought of refusing. The merchant had no right to order me. But then I reflected that a refusal would do no good, and might do harm, so without a word I entered the carriage.

The others were not slow to follow. Then Farmer Decker chirruped to Billy, and we rolled out of the farm yard and down the road.

But little was said on the way. I was busy with my own thoughts, and so were Mr. Woodward and Stumpy. The farmer asked several questions, but the merchant said he would learn all he wished to know at the judge's office, and this quieted him.

About five o'clock in the afternoon we rolled into Darbyville. While crossing the Pass River the sun had burst through the clouds, and now all was as bright and fresh as ever.

Judge Penfold's office was situated in the centre of the principal business block. When we arrived there we found a number of men standing about the door, no doubt discussing my escape, for they uttered many exclamations of surprise on seeing me.

Chief among them was Parsons, who looked pale and worried.

"Roger Strong!" he exclaimed. "Where have you been?"

"Took a walk for my health," I replied as lightly as I could, though my heart was heavy.

"Well, I guess we'll make sure it shan't happen again," he returned. "Hi, there, Booth! Here's your prisoner come back!"

In a moment the carpenter appeared upon the scene.

"You rascal, you!" he cried in angry tones. "A fine peck of trouble you've got yourself into!"

"What's all this about?" asked a heavy voice from the stairs, and Judge Penfold stood before me.

"I have brought your prisoner back, judge," replied Mr. Woodward.

"So I see. Well, Strong, what have you to say for yourself? Do you know breaking jail is a serious offence?"

"I don't know anything about it. I know I was locked up for nothing at all, and I escaped at the first chance offered."

"There was no chance offered at all, judge," broke in Booth, fearful of having a reflection cast upon his character. "He just went and ripped the hull floor up, that's what he did."

"Silence, Booth! Come upstairs and we will hear the particulars."

In a moment we were in Judge Penfold's office. I was told to take a seat on a bench, with Booth on one side of me and Parsons on the other.

Then Mr. Woodward introduced John Stumpy as a friend from San Antonio, Texas, and the two told their story, corroborated at its end by Farmer Decker, who trembled from head to foot at the idea of addressing as high a dignitary as Judge Penfold.

"What have you to say to this, Strong?" I was asked.

In a plain, straightforward way I told my story from beginning to end, told it in a manner that did not fail to impress nearly every one in the court-room but the judge and my accusers.

Of course Mr. Woodward and John Stumpy stoutly denied all I said, and their denial carried the day.

"Until we can have a real trial I will send you back to jail," said Judge Penfold.

"Why don't you send John Stumpy to jail, too?" I asked. "He is as much accused as I."

"We have only your word for that."

"Then let me send for my sister Kate and Dick Blair."

Judge Penfold rubbed his chin reflectively.

"I think I'll have to put you under bonds," he said to John Stumpy.

"Why so? The boy's word doesn't amount to anything," put in Mr. Woodward.

"Only a matter of form, Mr. Woodward. I will make it a thousand dollars. Will you go his bondsman?"

"Of course he will," said John Stumpy, hastily. "Won't you?"

The merchant winced. "I—I guess so," he stammered. "But

it's a strange proceeding."

In a few moments, by the aid of two other men, the bond was made out.

"I will make your bail a thousand dollars also," said Judge Penfold, turning to me. "I suppose it's quite useless though," he added sarcastically.

"Not quite so useless as you might think," exclaimed a hearty voice from the rear of the court-room.

I thought I recognized the tones, and turned hastily. There beside my sister Kate stood my uncle, Enos Moss, of whom I have already spoken.

He was a grizzly bearded sea-captain of seventy, with manner and speech suggestive the brine.

Breaking from Parsons and Booth, I ran to meet him. He shook both my hands and then clapped me on the shoulder.

"Cast up on a lee shore, are you, Roger?" he exclaimed. "And the wind a-blowing a hurricane."

"Yes, I am," I replied, "and I'm mighty glad you've come, Uncle Enos."

"Just dropped anchor in time," he went on. "Judge Penfold, do you remember me?"

"You are Carson Strong's brother-in-law, I believe?" replied the judge.

"You've hit it. Captain Enos Moss, part owner and sailing master of the Hattie Baker, as trim a craft as ever rounded the Horn. Been away for three years, and now on shore to stay."

"You're not going on any more voyages?" I queried.

"No, my hearty. I've made enough to keep me, and I'm getting too old to walk the quarter-deck. Besides, I've heard of your father's troubles from Kate, and I reckon they need sounding."

"Indeed they do."

"Well, now about your difficulty. A thousand-dollar bond, eh. It's pretty stiff, but I guess I can stand it."

"Thank you, sir," was all I could say.

"Don't say a word. Didn't your father put in a good word for me when I was a-courting your aunt that's dead and gone—God bless her! Indeed, he did! And I'll stand by you, Roger, no matter how hard the gale blows."

"Then you don't think I'm guilty?"

"What! a lad with your bearing a thief? Not much. The people in this village must be asleep—not to know better'n that?"

"Ahem!" coughed Judge Penfold, sternly. He considered my uncle's remarks decidedly impertinent. "Are you able to go his bail?" he asked.

"Reckon I am. I've just deposited ten thousand dollars in the bank here, and I've got twenty and more in New York. How will you have it—in cash?"

"A conditional check, certified, will do," replied Judge Penfold, shortly.

What he meant had to be explained, and then we all went to the banker's office. My uncle's account was found to be as he had stated, and about ten minutes later my bond was signed and I was at liberty to go where I pleased until called upon to appear.

Mr. Aaron Woodward and John Stumpy apparently did not relish the turn affairs had taken. But I paid no attention to them, and the business over, I hurried off with my sister and my newly arrived uncle.

"Did you find the statement?" I asked of Kate, as soon as we were out of hearing of the crowd.

"No, Roger, I looked and looked, but it wasn't anywhere, either at the tool house or on the way to Judge Penfold's."

"Have you heard from Mrs. Canby yet?"

"Yes, she is coming home."

"Does she blame me for what has happened?"

"She doesn't say."

"Never mind, Roger. We'll stick up for you," put in Uncle Enos, kindly.

I was considerably disturbed. What if Mrs. Canby should consider me at fault?

As we drew near to the cottage, I saw a lady standing by the gate, watching our approach. It was the Widow Canby.

# CHAPTER XVII

## A SUDDEN RESOLVE

My heart beat rapidly as I walked up to the gate. How would the good lady who had done so much for Kate and myself receive me?

An unkind word or an unfavorable insinuation from her would have hurt me worse than a thousand from any one else. She had been so generous that to have her turn would have made me feel as if I had lost my last friend on earth.

But as she had taken me in before when others had cast me out, so she now proved the friend in need.

"So they've thought better of it and set you free, Roger?" she said as I hurried up.

"Yes, Mrs. Canby," I returned. "I hope—I hope—" I began, and then came to a full stop.

"What?" and she caught my hand.

"I hope you don't think I had anything to do with the robbery," I stammered.

"No, Roger, I don't. I think you're an honest boy, and I've got to have more proof against you than I've heard yet before I'll believe otherwise."

"Thank you, ma'am, oh, thank you!" I blurted out, and the tears started to my eyes and rolled down my cheeks.

The events of which I am writing occurred several years ago, but I am not ashamed of those tears. They were the outcome of long-pent-up feelings, and I could not hold them back. My sister cried, too, and the Widow Canby and Uncle Enos looked very much as if they wished to join in.

"I knew you wouldn't think Roger did it," cried Kate. "I said all along you wouldn't, though everybody said you would."

"Folks don't appear to know me very well," returned Widow Canby, with a bit of grim humor in her tone. "I don't always think as others do. Come into the house and give me full particulars. Who is this man? Why, really! Captain Moss, I believe?"

"Yes, ma'am, Captain Moss—Roger's uncle, at your service," replied he, taking off his cap and bowing low. "I thought you'd remember me. Your husband as was once sailed to Boston with me."

"Oh, yes, I remember you. Will you come in?"

"Thank you, reckon I will. I have no home now, and hotels is scarce in Darbyville. I only arrived this noon, and I've been with Kate ever since. I must hunt up a boarding-house to stay at. Do you know of any close at hand?"

"Perhaps I do. Let us talk of that later on. I want to hear Roger's story first."

"Just as you say, ma'am. Only I must get a place to stop at to-night."

"You shall be provided for, Captain Moss. I have a spare room."

"You are very kind to an old sea-dog like myself, Mrs. Canby," said Uncle Enos.

The widow led the way into the dining room. The lamp was already lighted, and while my sister Kate busied herself with preparing supper, Mrs. Canby and my uncle sat down to listen to my story.

For the first time I told it with all the details that concerned myself,—how I had been waylaid by the Models, how Dick Blair had released me, what Stumpy had done at the tool house, and all, not forgetting about the statement Kate and I wished so much to find.

The Widow Canby and my uncle listened with close attention until I had finished.

"It's a strange story, Roger," said the widow, at its conclusion. "One hard to believe. But I know you tell the truth."

"What a rascal this Woodward must be!" broke in my uncle "He's a far greater villain in his way than this John Stumpy. I am strongly inclined to figure that you're right, and he is the one that ran your father up on a lee shore."

"I don't think father did a single thing that was wrong—that is, knowingly," I returned. "If he did do wrong, I'm sure Mr. Woodward made it appear as if it was all right."

"No doubt, no doubt. If you could only get to the bottom of this Weaver's statement."

"And when is this trial to come off?" put in Mrs. Canby. "Really I don't see what good it will do me if this man has lost the money."

"I'd like to find that, too," I returned.

Presently Kate announced that supper was ready, and we all sat down. The widow said that she had found her sister much better, and on receiving Kate's letter had started for her home at once. The loss of the money did not disturb her as much as I had anticipated, and as every one was hungry, the meal passed off tolerably well.

When we had nearly finished there was a knock on the door, and Kate admitted Mr. Woodward's errand boy. He had a note for me. It contained but a single sentence:—

"Please call at my house this evening about nine o'clock."

I read the note over with interest, and then informed the others of what it contained.

"Shall you go?" asked Kate, anxiously.

"I suppose I might."

"Maybe it's a plot," suggested the widow.

"Might waylay you," added Uncle Enos. "A man like him is liable to do 'most anything."

"I don't think he would dare do me any bodily injury," I replied. "He would know I had told some one where I was going, and that my absence would be noticed."

"If you go, take me in tow," said my uncle. "I needn't go in with you, but I can hang around outside, and if anything goes wrong, all you've got to do is to holler like all creation, and I'll come to the rescue."

"Oh, if Roger runs any risk, I'd rather he wouldn't go," exclaimed Kate, in alarm.

"I don't think the risk is very great," I returned. "Besides, I may find the missing statement. That is worth trying for."

"I shall be in dread until you return," she replied, with a grave shake of her head.

"When will you start?" asked Uncle Enos.

"About half past eight. It won't take over half an hour to reach his house."

We continued to discuss Mr. Woodward for some time, and also the action of the Models and what I should do on their score. My Uncle Enos was for prosecuting them, but the Widow Canby said that the future would bring its own punishment, and on this we rested.

"And now about my board," began Uncle Enos, during a dull in the conversation. "I must find a boarding-house for after to-night."

"Wouldn't you like to stay with the children?" asked Mrs. Canby.

"Yes, ma'am; indeed I would. To tell the truth, it's my intention sooner or later to offer them a home with me."

"I should hate to have them leave me," returned the widow, quickly.

"I suppose so."

"How would you like to board with me? As I have said, there is lots of room, and you have just eaten a sample meal. We do not live in style—but—"

"Plenty good enough style," interrupted Captain Enos, "and better grub then we had on the Hattie Baker, I'll be bound. I'd like it first rate here if the terms wasn't too high."

"What do you think fair?"

"I'm sure I don't know, ma'am. I haven't paid a week's board in three years."

"Would five dollars a week be too much?"

"No, ma'am. Are you sure it's enough? I don't want to crowd your hospitality."

"I'd be satisfied with five dollars. Of course boarders are out of my line, but there are exceptions to all cases. Besides, I'll feel safer with another man about the house. No reflection on you, Roger, but you won't always be here together."

"No, ma'am," replied my uncle. "I must visit my brother-in-law at the prison—that will take several days."

"Will you take me with you?" asked Kate, eagerly.

"Certainly, and you, too, Roger, if you want to go."

"I would like to very much," was my reply. "But I want to

ask even a bigger favor than that, Uncle Enos."

"Yes?"

"Yes, sir. You may think it a good deal, but you've been so kind, and I haven't any one else to go to."

"Well, what is it, my boy? I'll do it if I can."

"Lend me about fifty dollars."

My Uncle Enos raised his eyebrows in surprise.

"Fifty dollars?" he repeated.

"Yes, sir. That is, if you can spare it. I'll promise to pay it back some day."

"And what do you intend to do with it?"

"I want to go to Chicago, sir."

"To Chicago?"

All three of my listeners repeated the words in chorus; then Captain Enos continued:—

"And what are you going to do there?"

"I want to hunt up this Holtzmann, and find out what he knows about my father's affairs. I'm satisfied that he is as deep in it as Mr. Woodward or John Stumpy, and if I can only by some means get him to tell what he knows, I may accomplish a good deal."

My Uncle Enos put his hand upon my shoulder;  "Well,

Roger, you're a brave boy, and I'll trust you. You shall have fifty dollars, and a hundred, if you want it, to do as you think best. Only don't get into trouble."

"Thank you Uncle Enos, thank you!" I cried heartily. "Some day I'll pay you back."

"I don't want it back, my lad. If you can catch any proofs that will help clear your father, I shall be more than satisfied."

"And when shall you go?" asked Kate.

"I don't know. It will depend on my interview with Mr. Woodward and also on what John Stumpy does. Not inside of several days, at least. Besides, we want to see father first, you know."

"Of course."

"We can go to Trenton tomorrow," said Uncle Enos. At Trenton was located the State prison. After consulting a time table printed in the Darbyville Record, we found we could catch a train for that city at 8.25 from Newville the next morning, and this we decided to take.

Having settled this matter, we returned again to the discussion of the incidents surrounding the robbery, and what would probably be the next movements of those fighting against me. Uncle Enos grew greatly interested, and said he knew a lawyer in New York who might secure some good private detective who could take the case in hand.

Finally it came half past eight, and putting on my hat, I started for Mr. Woodward's residence.

# CHAPTER XVIII

## IN MR. WOODWARD'S LIBRARY

Though outwardly calm, I was considerably agitated as I walked to Darbyville. Why the merchant had sent for me I could not surmise. Of course it was on account of the robbery, but so far as I knew both of us had taken a separate stand, and neither would turn back. I thought it barely possible that he wished to intimidate me into receding from my position. He was as much of a bully in his way as Duncan, and would not hesitate to use every means in his power to bring me to terms.

Arriving at Mr. Woodward's house, I ascended the steps and rang the bell.

"Is Mr. Woodward in?" I asked of the girl who answered the summons.

"I'll see, sir," she replied. "Who shall I say it is?"

"Roger Strong."

The girl left me standing in the hall. While waiting for her return I could not help but remember the old lines:—

"'Will you walk into my parlor?'
Said the spider to the fly."

But if I was walking into the spider's parlor, it would be my own fault if I got hurt, for I was entering with my eyes open. I determined to be on my guard, and take nothing for granted.

"Mr. Woodward will be pleased to see you in his library," said the girl upon her return, and then, having indicated the door, she vanished down the back hall.

As I put my hand upon the door-knob, I heard steps upon the stairs, and looking up saw Duncan Woodward descending.

His face was still swollen from the punishment I had inflicted upon him. Nevertheless, he was faultlessly dressed in full evening costume, and I rightly conjectured he was going to spend the night in some fashionable dissipation such as dancing or card-playing.

"Hello! how did you get in here?" he exclaimed.

"Was let in," was my mild reply, not caring to pick a quarrel with him.

"Was, eh? And what for, I'd like to know?"

"That's your father's business, Duncan."

"Don't Duncan me any more, Roger Strong. What's my father's business?"

"What I came for. He sent for me."

"Oh, he did. Reckon he's going to square accounts with you."

"I don't know what accounts he's going to square," I went on in curiosity.

"Didn't you as much as try to intimate he was lying—down in Judge Penfold's court this afternoon?"

"I only told what I knew to be the truth," I replied calmly.

"The truth. Humph! I believe you took the widow's money yourself."

"Take care what you're saying," I replied angrily. "I don't propose to stand any such talk from you."

Duncan grew speechless. "Why, you—you—" he began.

"Hold up now before you say something that you'll be sorry for. This is your house, but you have no right to insult me in it."

"Quite right, Strong, quite right." The library door had opened, and Mr. Woodward stood upon the threshold, gazing sharply at his son. "Strong is here upon my invitation, Duncan; you ought to treat him with more politeness," he added.

If Duncan was amazed at this speech, so was I. The merchant taking my part? What did it mean?

"Why, I—I—" began Duncan, but he could really get no further.

"No explanation is necessary," interrupted his father, coolly.

"Strong, please step in, will you?"

"Yes, sir," and I suited the action to the word.

As I did so Duncan passed on to the front door.

"I'll get even with you yet, you cad!" he muttered under his breath; but I paid no attention to his words. I had "bigger fish to fry."

Once inside of Mr. Woodward's library, the merchant closed the door behind me and then invited me to take a seat beside his desk, at the same time throwing himself back in his easy chair.

"I suppose you thought it rather singular that I should send for you," he said by way of an opening.

"Yes, sir, I did," was all I could reply.

"I thought as much. It was only an impulse of mine, sir, only an impulse. I wished to see if we cannot arrange this—this little difficulty without publicity. I would rather lose a good deal, yes, sir, a good deal, than have my name dragged into court."

"All I ask is for justice," I replied calmly. "I am under arrest for a crime of which I am innocent. On the other hand, you are trying to shield a man I know is guilty."

I expected a storm of indignation from Mr. Woodward because of the last remark. Yet he showed no sign of resentment.

"Don't you think you might be mistaken in your identification of Mr. Stumpy?" he replied, and I noticed that again he nearly stumbled in pronouncing the tramp's name.

"No, sir," I replied promptly.

"Remember that you saw him only by lantern light, and then but for a few minutes."

"I saw him by daylight as well."

"When?"

"In the morning. He came as a beggar."

"A beggar? Impossible!" The merchant held, up his hands in assumed amazement. "Why, Strong, the idea of Mr. Stumpy begging is ridiculous."

"Just the same it is true, Mr. Woodward. And what is more, he is the thief, and you know it."

"That's a strong assertion to make, sir, a very strong assertion."

"Nevertheless, I believe I can prove my words."

Mr. Woodward turned slightly pale.

"You can prove no such thing," he cried.

"Yes, I can. Didn't Stumpy admit he had taken the money?"

"Never, sir."

"He did."

"When?"

"This afternoon while you were at Decker's place."

Had I slapped the merchant in the face he would not have been more surprised. He sprang to his feet and glared at me.

"You—you—Who says he made such an admission?"

"I say so."

"Ah! I see, you were spying on us. You rascal!"

"It strikes me that you are the rascal," I returned. "You try deliberately to shield a thief."

"What!"

"Yes, it's true."

"Can you prove it?"

Mr. Woodward asked the question sneeringly, but there was much of curiosity in his tones.

"Perhaps I can."

The merchant pulled his mustache nervously.

"Strong, you are greatly mistaken. But don't let us quarrel any more."

"I don't want to quarrel."

"I feel badly over the whole affair, and Mr. Stumpy is fairly sick. I suppose you think you are right, but you are mistaken. Now I have a proposition to make to you." Mr. Woodward leaned forward in his chair. "Suppose you admit that you are mistaken—that Mr. Stumpy is not the man? Do this, and I will not prosecute you for having taken my papers."

I was surprised and indignant; surprised that Mr. Woodward should still insist upon my having taken his papers, and indignant because of his outrageous offer.

"Mr. Woodward," I began firmly, "you can prosecute me or not; Stumpy is the guilty man, and I shall always stick to it."

"Then you will go to jail, too."

"For the last time let me say I have not seen your papers."

"It is false. You took them from this room last night. At the very time you pretend you were after the robber at Mrs. Canby's house you were here ransacking my desk."

"Mr. Woodward—"

"There is no use in denying it. I have abundant proofs. The girl who cleaned up here this morning found a handkerchief with your name on it lying on the floor. If you weren't here, how did that come here?"

"My handkerchief?"

"Yes, sir, your handkerchief; and Mary O'Brien can identify it and tell where she found it."

"Some one else must have had it," I stammered, and then suddenly: "I know who the party is—Duncan."

"Duncan!"

"Yes, sir. He took that handkerchief away from me when the Models waylaid me!"

"My son! Really, Strong, you are mad! But I will take you  in hand, sir; yes, indeed, I will."

"No, you won't, Aaron Woodward!" I cried, for once letting my temper get the better of me. "You are awfully cunning, but I am not afraid of you. I am willing to have all these matters sifted to the bottom, and the sooner the better. What papers have you missed? Were they the ones that Holtzmann of Chicago is after? How is it that my father is in prison while you live in style on money you never earned? Who is the relative that left it to you? Did you ever make a clear statement concerning the transactions that took away my father's honest name?"

"Stop! Stop!"

"I will not stop! You want an investigation; so do I. Luckily my uncle, Captain Enos Moss, has just returned from a voyage. He has quite some money, and I know he will use it to bring the guilty parties to justice. And then—"

I did not finish. Mr. Woodward had strode over to the door and locked it, putting the key in his pocket.

"You know too much, Strong," he muttered between his set teeth, as he caught me by the collar; "too much entirely. We must come to a settlement before you leave this room."

# CHAPTER XIX

## A CLEVER RUSE

I must confess I was frightened when Mr. Woodward locked the door of his library and caught me by the collar. Was it possible that he contemplated doing me physical harm? It looked that way.

I was not accustomed to such rough treatment, and I resented it instantly. I was not very large for my age, but I was strong, and ducking my head I wrenched myself free from his grasp and sprang to the other side of the small table that stood in the centre of the room.

"What do you mean by treating me in this manner!" I cried. "Unlock that door at once!"

"Not much, sir," replied Mr. Woodward, vehemently. "You've made some remarkable statements, young man, and I demand a clear explanation before you leave."

"Well, you demand too much, Aaron Woodward," I replied firmly. "Unlock that door."

"Not just yet. I want to know what you know of Holtzmann of Chicago?"

"You won't learn by treating me in this manner," was my determined reply. "Unlock that door, or, take my word for it, I'll arouse the whole neighborhood."

"You'll do nothing of the kind, young man," he rejoined.

"I will."

"Make the least disturbance and you shall pay dearly for it. Understand, sir, I'm not to be trifled with."

"And I'm not to be frightened into submission," I returned with spirit. "I have a right to leave when I please and I shall do so."

"Not till I am ready," said he, coolly.

I was nonplussed and alarmed—nonplussed over the question of how to get away, and alarmed at the thought of what might happen if I was compelled to remain.

I began to understand Mr. Aaron Woodward's true character. Like Duncan, he was not only a bully, but also a brute. Words having failed, he was now evidently going to see what physical force could accomplish.

"Forewarned is forearmed" is an old saying, and now I applied it to myself. In other words, I prepared for an encounter. On the centre table lay a photograph album. It was thick and heavy and capable of proving quite a formidable article of defence. I picked it up, and stepping behind a large easy chair, stood on my guard.

Seeing the action, the merchant paused.

"What are going to do with that?" he asked.

"You'll see if you keep on," I replied. "I don't intend to stand this much longer. You had better open the door."

"You think you're a brainy boy, Strong," he sneered.

"I've got too much brain to let you ride over me."

"You think you have a case against me and Mr. Stumpy, and you intend to drag it into court and make a great fuss over it," he went on.

"I'm going to get back my father's honest name."

"What you mean is that you intend to drag my name in the mire," he stormed.

"You can have it so, if you please."

"I shall not allow it. You, a young upstart!"

"Take care, Mr. Woodward!"

"Do you think I will submit to it?" He glared at me and threw a hasty glance around the room. "Not much!"

Suddenly he stepped to the windows and pulled down the shades. Then he took out his watch and looked at the time. I wondered what he was up to now. I was not long in finding out.

"Listen to me," he said in a low, intense tone, "We are alone in this house—you and I—and will be for half an hour or more. You are in my power. What will you do? Give up all the papers you possess and promise to keep silent about what you know or take the consequences."

It would be telling an untruth to say I was not thoroughly startled by the merchant's sudden change of manner. He was about to assault me, that was plain to see, and he wished me to understand that no one was near either to assist me or to bear witness against his dark doings.

I must fight my own battles, not only in a war of words, but also in a war of blows. I was not afraid after the first shock was over. My cause was a just one, and I would stand by it, no matter what the consequences might be.

"I don't fear you, Aaron Woodward," I replied, as steadily as I could. "I am in the right and shall stick up for it, no matter what comes."

"You defy me?" he cried in a rage.

"Yes, I do."

I had hardly uttered the words before he caught up a heavy cane standing beside his desk and made for me. There was a wicked determination in his eyes, and I could see that all the evil passions within him were aroused.

"We'll see who is master here," he went on.

"Stand back!" I cried. "Don't come a step nearer! If you do, you'll be sorry for it!"

He paid no attention to my warning, but kept on advancing, raising the cane over his head as he did so.

When he was within three feet of me he aimed a blow at my head. Had he hit me, I am certain he would have cracked my skull open.

Edward Stratemeyer

But I was too quick for him, I dodged, and the cane struck the back of the chair.

Before he could recover from his onslaught I hurled the album at him with all force. It struck him full in the face, and must have loosened several of his teeth, for he put his hand up to his mouth as he reeled over backward.

I was not astonished. I had accomplished just what I had set out to do. My one thought now was to make my escape. How was it to be done?

The key to the door was in the merchant's pocket, and this I could, not obtain. The windows were closed, and the blinds drawn down.

I had but an instant to think. Spluttering to himself, my assailant was endeavoring to rise to his feet.

A hasty glance around the room revealed a door partly hidden by a curtain next the mantelpiece. Where it led to I did not know, but concluding that any place would be better than to remain in the library, I tried the door, found it open, and slipped out.

"Stop, stop!" roared Mr. Woodward. "Stop, this instant!"

But I did not stop. I found myself in the dining room, and at once put the long table between us.

"Don't you come any nearer," I called out sharply. "If you do, it may be at the cost of your life."

As I spoke I picked up a fancy silver knife that lay on the table. It had a rough resemblance to a pocket pistol, and gave me the idea of palming it off as such.

"Would you shoot me?" cried the merchant, in sudden terror, as he saw what he supposed was the barrel of a revolver pointed at his head.

"Why shouldn't I?" was the reply. "You have no right to detain me."

"I don't want to detain you. I only want to come to a settlement," he returned lamely.

"And I want nothing more to do with you. I'll give you one minute to show me the way to the front door."

"Yes, but, Strong—"

"No more talk, if you please. Do you intend to show me the way out, or shall I fire?"

Then Mr. Aaron Woodward showed what a coward he really was. He gave a cry of horror and sank completely out of sight.

"Don't shoot, Strong. I pray you, take care. I'll show you the way out, indeed I will!"

"Well, hurry about it. I don't intend to stand any more nonsense."

"Here, this way. Please stop pointing that pistol at me; it might go off, you know."

"Then the sooner you show me the way out, the better for you," I returned coolly, inwardly amused at his sudden change of manner

"This way, then. I—I trust you will keep this—this little

meeting of ours a secret."

"Why should I?"

"Because it—it would do no good to have it made public."

"I'll see about it," was my reply.

By this time we had reached the front door, and with unwilling hands the merchant opened it.

"Now stand aside and let me pass," I commanded.

"I will. But, Strong—"

"No more words are needed," I returned. "I have had enough of you, Mr. Aaron Woodward. The next time you hear from me it will be in quite a different shape."

"What do you mean?" he cried, in sudden alarm.

"You will find out soon enough. In the meantime let me return your fancy knife. I have no further use for it."

I tossed the article over. He looked at it and then at me. Clearly he was mad enough to "chew me up." Bidding him a mocking good night, I ran down the steps and hurried away.

# CHAPTER XX

## AT THE PRISON

Mr. Woodward's actions had aroused me as I had never been aroused before. My eyes were wide open at last. I realized that if I ever expected to gain our family rights I must fight for them—and fight unflinchingly to the bitter end.

It was nearly ten o'clock when I reached the Widow Canby's house. I met my Uncle Enos on the porch. He had grown impatient, and was about to start for Darbyville in search of me.

In the dining room I told my story. All laughed heartily at the ruse I had played upon the merchant, but were indignant at the treatment I had received.

"Wish I'd been with you," remarked my uncle, with a vigorous shake of his head. "I'd a-smashed in his figurehead, keelhaul me if I wouldn't!"

"What do you intend to do now?" asked Kate.

"Let's see; to-day is Friday. If you will take us to Trenton to-morrow, Uncle Enos, I'll start for Chicago on Monday."

"Don't you think you had better have this Woodward arrested first?" asked Captain Enos.

"No; I would rather let him think that for the present I had dropped the whole matter. It may throw him off his guard and enable me to pick up more clews against him."

"That's an idea. Roger, you've got a level head on your shoulders, and we can't do any better than follow your advice," returned my uncle.

I did but little sleeping that night. For a long time I lay awake thinking over my future actions. Then when I did fall into a doze my rest was broken by dreams of the fire at the tool house and Mr. Woodward's attack.

I was up at five o'clock in the morning, attending to the regular chores. I did not know who would do them during my absence, and as soon as the widow appeared I spoke to her on the subject.

"Your uncle mentioned the matter last night," said Mrs. Canby. "He said he would do all that was required until you came back. He doesn't want to remain idle all day, and thought the work would just suit him."

This was kind of Uncle Enos, and I told him so when an hour later he appeared, dressed in his best, his trunk having arrived the evening before.

"Yes, Roger, I'd rather do it than sit twirling my thumbs, a-waiting for you to come back," said he. "I used to do such work years ago, before I shipped on the Anna Siegel, and to do it again will make me feel like a boy once more. But come; let's go to mess and then hoist anchor and away."

A few minutes later we were at breakfast. Then I put on my good clothes and brought around the horse and carriage, for the Widow Canby insisted upon driving us down to Newville by way of Darbyville just to show folks, as she said, that she had not lost confidence in me.

Kate was in a flutter of excitement. She had wished to see my father every day since he had been taken away. As for myself, I was fully as impatient. My father was very dear to me, and every time I thought of him I prayed that God would place it within my power to clear his name from the stain that now rested upon him.

We reached the station in Newville five minutes before train time. My uncle procured our tickets and also checked the basket of delicacies the Widow Canby had prepared.

"Remember me to Mr. Strong," said the widow, as we boarded the train. "Tell him I don't believe he's guilty, and perhaps other people in Darbyville won't think so either before long."

A moment later and we were off. Kate and Uncle Enos occupied one seat, and I sat directly behind them. A ride of an hour followed, and finally, after crossing a number of other railroads, we rolled into a brick station, and the conductor sang out:—

"Trenton!"

It was eleven o'clock when we crossed the wooden foot-bridge of the station and emerged upon the street.

"We'll go to the prison at once," said my uncle. "Perhaps it isn't 'visiting day,' as they call it, but I reckon I can fix it. Sailors on shore have special privileges," he added with a laugh.

"Which way is it?" asked Kate.

"I don't know. We'll take a carriage and trust to the driver."

He called a coach, and soon we were rolling off.

Finally the coach stopped, and the driver sprang from his box.

"Here you are, sir," he said, as he opened the door.

I looked up at the big stone buildings before us. My father was behind those walls. I glanced at Kate. The poor girl was in tears.

"You had better stay on board here till I go in and take soundings," said Captain Enos. "I won't be gone long."

Jumping to the pavement, he walked up to the big open door and entered.

"What a dreadful place!" said my sister, as she strained her eyes to catch sight of some prisoner.

My uncle was gone not over ten minutes, yet the wait seemed an age. He returned with a brightened face.

"I had hard work to get permission, but we are to have half an hour's talk with your father under the supervision of a deputy," he explained.

In another moment we were inside. We walked along a wide corridor and into an office, and then a short, stout man, Mr. Carr, the deputy, joined us.

"This way, please," he said, and gave a kindly glance at Kate and myself. "You will have to leave the basket here. I will see that it reaches the—the—your father."

He led the way. How my heart beat! Why, I cannot tell.

"I'll go in first," said my Uncle Enos.

We entered a room. In a moment the deputy brought in a man dressed in striped clothing, and with his hair cut close. It was my father.

My uncle and I rushed forward. But we were too late. With a cry Kate was in his arms. It was a great moment all around.

"My children! My Katie and my Roger!" was all my father could say, but the words went straight home.

"I am heartily glad that you are back," he said then to my uncle. "You will look after them, Enos, until I am free."

"Indeed I will," replied Captain Enos, heartily. "But you must listen to Roger. He has a long story to tell."

"Then tell it. I am dying to hear news from home." We sat down, and I told my story. Perhaps the deputy ought not to have allowed me to say all I did, but he pretended not to hear.

My father listened with keen attention to every word, and as I went on, his eyes grew brighter and brighter.

"Roger, my faithful boy, you almost make me hope for freedom," he cried. "Oh, how I long to be set right before the world!"

"God make it so," put in my uncle, solemnly. "To suffer unjustly is terrible."

Then I told of my interview with Mr. Woodward in his library and of Holtzmann.

"Holtzmann was one of the principal witnesses against me," said my father. "So was Nicholas Weaver, who managed the Brooklyn business for Holland & Mack. Who John Stumpy can be I do not know. Perhaps I would if I saw him face to face. There was another man—he was quite bald, with a red blotch on the front of his hand—who was brought forward by Woodward to prove that he had nothing to do with the presentation of the forged checks and notes, but what his name was I have forgotten."

"This can't be the man, for he has a heavy head of hair," I replied. "But I am sure Stumpy is not his true name."

"Probably not. Well, Roger, do your best, not only for me but for Katie's sake and your own."

Then the conversation became general, and all too soon the half hour was at an end. My father sent his regards to Mrs. Canby, with many thanks for the basket of delicacies, and then with a kiss for Kate and a shake of the hand to Uncle Enos and me, we parted.

Little was said on the way back. No one cared to go to a restaurant, and we took the first train homeward.

It was dark when we reached Newville. The Widow Canby's carriage was at the depot waiting for us.

"Suppose I get my ticket for Chicago now," said I. "It will save time Monday, and I can find out all about the train."

"A good idea," returned my uncle. "I'll go with you."

So while Kate joined Mrs. Canby we entered the depot.

The ticket was soon in my possession, and then I asked the ticket seller a number of questions concerning the route and the time I would reach my destination.

Suddenly instinct prompted me to turn quickly. I did so and found John Stumpy at my shoulder.

# CHAPTER XXI

## A MIDNIGHT ADVENTURE

Mr. John Stumpy had evidently been watching my proceedings closely, for when I turned to him he was quite startled. However, it did not take him long to recover, and then, bracing up, he hurried away without a word.

He was now neatly dressed and had had his face shaved. I conjectured that Mr. Woodward had advised this change in order to more fully carry out the deception in relation to the tramp's real character.

"There's that Stumpy," I whispered to Captain Enos, as I pointed my finger at the man. "He has been watching us."

"How do you know?" asked my uncle.

"Because he was just looking over my shoulder," I replied. "Shall I speak to him? I'd like to know what he intends to do next."

"It won't do any good. It ain't likely he'd tell you anything, and if he did, it wouldn't be the truth."

"Maybe it might."

"Well, do as you think best, Roger, only don't be too long—the widow and Kate are waiting, you know."

Pushing through the crowd, I tapped Stumpy on the shoulder. He looked around in assumed surprise.

"Hullo!" he exclaimed sharply. "What do you want?"

"Nothing much," I returned. "I just saw you were greatly interested in what I was doing."

"Why, I didn't see you before."

"You were just looking over my shoulder."

"You're mistaken, young man, just as you are in several other things."

"I'm not mistaken in several other things."

"What do you intend to do?" he asked curiously.

"That's my business."

"Where have you been?"

"That is my business also."

"Strong, you're a fool," he whispered. "Do you think you can hurt men like Mr. Woodward and myself?"

"I can bring you to justice."

"Bah! I suppose you think you can do wonders by going to Chicago."

"How do you know I am going to Chicago?" I questioned quickly.

Stumpy's face fell, as he realized the slip he had made.

"Never mind. But you won't gain anything," he went on. "Better stay home and save your money."

And to avoid further talk he pushed his way through the crowd and was lost to sight.

A moment later I joined the others in the carriage. While driving home I related the conversation recorded above.

"It's too bad he found out you were going to Chicago," said my uncle. "He may try to stop you."

"I'll keep my eyes open," I replied.

The remainder of the day was spent in active work around the widow's place. Not only did I labor all the afternoon, but far into the evening as well, to show that I did not intend to shirk my duty even though I was going away. Besides, Mrs. Canby had treated me so well that I was almost willing to work my fingers to the bone to serve her.

The following day was Sunday. Kate and I were in the habit of attending church and Sunday-school over in Darbyville, but we shrank from doing so now. But Uncle Enos and I went to church, and despite the many curious eyes levelled at me, I managed to give attention to an excellent sermon. I noticed that the Woodward pew was empty, but then this was of common occurrence and excited no comment.

On Sunday evening my handbag stood in my room packed, ready for my departure. Dick Blair came over to see me and brought strange and sad news.

Duncan Woodward and Pultzer, his intimate crony, had gotten into a row in a pool room down in Newville and were both under arrest. Mr. Woodward and Mr. Pultzer had gone off to get their sons out of jail. Dick did not know how the row had started, but had heard that the young men had been drinking heavily.

I was much shocked at the news, and so were the others. If affairs kept on like this, Mr. Aaron Woodward would certainly have his hands full.

I retired early so as to be on hand the next day. Sleep was out of the question. I had never been a hundred miles away from Darbyville, and the prospect of leaving filled me with excitement.

I was up long before it was necessary, but found Kate ahead of me.

"You're going to have a good, hot breakfast before you go," she said. "Sit right down. It's all ready."

Presently, as I was eating, my uncle and Mrs. Canby joined me. They were full of advice as to what to do and what to avoid, and I listened to all they had to say attentively.

But all things must come to an end, and at length breakfast was over. My Uncle Enos and Kate drove me to Newville, and waited till the train rolled in.

"Good-by, Roger," said Kate. "Please, please, now do keep out of trouble."

"I will, Kate," I returned, and kissed her. Then I shook hands with my uncle.

"Keep a clear weather eye and a strong hand at the wheel, Roger, my boy," he said, "and you'll make port all safe."

"I'll try, Uncle Enos."

A moment more and I was on the cars. Then with an "All aboard" the conductor gave the signal, and the train moved off.

I passed into the car and took a vacant seat near the centre. I had hardly sat down before a well-dressed stranger took the seat beside me.

"Hot day," said he, after he had arranged his bag on the floor beside my own.

"Yes, it is," I replied, "and dry, too."

"Meanest part of the country I've struck yet," he went on. "Don't have any such climate as this out West."

"I should think that would depend on where you come from," I returned, with a short laugh.

"I hail from Chicago. It's hot there, but we get plenty of breeze from the lakes."

I looked at the man with some attention. He came from the city I intended to visit, and perhaps he might give me some information.

He was a burly man of middle age, and, as I have said, well dressed, though a trifle loud. His hair was black, as was also his mustache, which he continually kept smoothing down with one hand. I did not like his looks particularly, nor his tone of voice. They reminded me strongly of some one, but whom I could not remember.

"You come from Chicago," I said. "I am going there."

"Is that so? Then we can travel together. I like to have some one going along, don't you?"

I felt like saying that that would depend on who the some one was, but thinking this would hardly be polite, I returned:—

"I don't know. I've never travelled before."

"No? Well, it's fun at first, but you soon get tired of it. My name is Allen Price; what is yours?"

"Roger Strong."

"Glad to meet you." He extended his hand. "You're rather young to be travelling alone—that is, going a distance. Do you smoke? We'll go into the smoker and take it easy. I have some prime cigars."

"Thank you, I don't smoke."

"That's too bad. Nothing like a good cigar to quiet a man's nerves when he's riding. So you're going to Chicago? On a visit?"

"No, sir; on business."

"Yes? Rather young for business—excuse me for saying so."

"It is a personal business."

"Oh, I see. Going to claim a dead uncle's property or something like that, I suppose. Ha! ha! well, I wish you luck."

Mr. Allen Price rattled on in this fashion for some time, and at length I grew interested in the man in spite of myself. I was positive I had seen him before, but where I could not tell. I asked him if he had ever been to Darbyville.

"Never heard of the place," he replied. "Only been in Jersey a month, and that time was spent principally in Jersey City and Camden. I'm in the pottery business. Our principal office is in Chicago."

"Do you know much about that city?"

"Lived there all my life."

I was on the point of asking him about Holtzmann, but on second thought decided to remain silent.

On and on sped the train, making but few stops. There was a dining-car attached but I was travelling on a cheap scale, and made my dinner and supper from the generous lunch the widow had provided.

Mr. Price went to the dining-car and also the smoker. He returned about nine o'clock in the evening, just as I was falling into a light doze.

"Thought I'd get a sleeper," he explained. "But they are all full, so I'll have to snooze beside you here."

His breath smelt strongly of liquor, but I had no right to object, and he dropped heavily into the seat.

Presently I went sound asleep. How long I slept I do not

know. When I awoke it was with a sharp, stinging sensation in the head. A pungent odor filled my nose, the scent coming from a handkerchief some one had thrown over my face.

With a gasp I pulled the handkerchief aside and sat up. Beside me sat Mr. Allen Price with my handbag on his lap. He had a number of keys in his hand and was trying to unlock the bag.

Edward Stratemeyer

# CHAPTER XXII

## A TELEGRAM

I was startled and indignant when I discovered Mr. Allen Price with my handbag, trying to open it. It looked very much as if my fellow-passenger was endeavoring to rob me.

I had suspected from the start that this man was not "straight." There was that peculiar something about his manner which I did not like. He had been altogether too familiar from the first; too willing to make himself agreeable.

What he expected to find in my bag I could not imagine. If his mission was robbery pure and simple, why had he not selected some one who looked richer than myself? There was, I am certain, nothing about me to make him believe I had anything of great value in the bag.

"What are you doing with my valise?" I demanded as I straightened up.

My sudden question made the man almost jump to his feet. The bag dropped from his lap to the floor, and the keys in his hand jingled after it.

"I—I—didn't think you were awake," he stammered.

"You didn't?" I repeated, puzzled as to what to say.

"No—I—I—"

"You were trying to open my bag."

"So I was—but it's all a mistake, I assure you."

"A mistake?"

"Quite a mistake, Strong." He cleared his throat. "The fact is, I'm suffering so from the toothache that I'm hardly able to judge of what I'm doing. I thought your bag was my own."

"They are not much alike," I returned bluntly.

"Well, you see mine is a new one, and I'm not used to it yet. I hope you don't think I was trying to rob you?" he went on, with a look of reproach.

I was silent. I did think that that was just what he was trying to do, but I hardly cared to say so.

"It's awful to have such toothaches as I get," he continued, putting his hand to his cheek. "They come on me unawares, and drive me frantic. I wanted to get my teeth attended to in Jersey City when I was there, but I didn't have time."

"What's this on the handkerchief?" I asked.

"Oh, I guess I spilled some of my toothache cure on it," he replied, after some hesitation. "I used some and then put the bottle back in the valise. That's how I came to look for the bottle again. I hope you're not offended. It was all a mistake."

"It's all right if that's the case," I returned coolly.

Holding my valise on my lap, I settled back in the seat again, but not to sleep. The little adventure had aroused me thoroughly. Mr. Allen Price sat beside me for a few moments in silence.

"Guess I'll go into the smoker," he said finally, as he rose. "Maybe a cigar will help me," and taking up his handbag, he walked down the aisle.

In a dreamy way I meditated over what had occurred. I could not help but think that the handkerchief I had found spread over my face had been saturated with chloroform, and that my fellow-passenger had endeavored to put me in a sound sleep and then rifle my bag. Of course I might be mistaken, but still I was positive that Mr. Allen Price would bear watching.

About four o'clock in the morning the train came to a sudden stop. The jar was so pronounced that it woke nearly all of the passengers.

Thinking that possibly we had arrived at our destination, I raised the window and peered out.

Instead of being in the heart of a city, however, I soon discovered we were in a belt of timber land. Huge trees lined the road on both sides, and ahead I could hear the flowing of a mountain stream.

The train hands were out with their lanterns, and by their movements it was plain to see that something was up.

I waited in my seat for ten minutes or more, and then as a number of passengers left the car, I took up my bag and did the same.

A walk to the front of the train soon made known the cause of the delay. Over a small mountain stream a strong wooden bridge with iron frame had been built. Near the bridge grew a number of tall trees, and one of these had been washed loose by the water and overturned in such a manner that the largest branch blocked the progress of the locomotive. The strong headlight had revealed the state of affairs to the engineer, and he had stopped within five feet of the obstruction. Had he run on, it is impossible to calculate what amount of damage might have been done.

"Don't see what we are going to do, except to run back to Smalleyville," said the engineer, who was in consultation with the conductor.

"Can't we roll the tree out of the way?" asked the latter official.

The engineer shook his head.

"Too heavy. All the men on the train couldn't budge it."

They stood in silence for a moment.

"If you had a rope, you could make the engine haul it," I suggested to the fireman, who was a young fellow.

"A good idea," he exclaimed, and reported it to his superior.

"First-class plan; but we haven't got the rope," said the engineer.

"Have you got an axe?"

"Yes."

"Then why not chop it off?"

"That's so! Larry, bring the axes."

"It won't do any good," said one of the brakemen who had just come up. "The bridge has shifted."

An examination proved his assertion to be correct. As soon as this became known, a danger light was hung at either end of the structure, and then we started running backward to Smalleyville.

"How long will this delay us?" I asked of the conductor as he came through, explaining matters.

"I can't tell. Perhaps only a few hours, perhaps more. It depends on how soon the wrecking gang arrive on the spot. As soon as they get there, they will go right to work, and it won't take them long to fix matters up."

Smalleyville proved to be a small town of not over five hundred inhabitants. There was quite an excitement around the depot when the train came in, and despatches were sent in various directions.

Presently a shower came up, and this drove the passengers to the cars and the station. I got aboard the train at first to listen to what the train hands might have to say. I found one of the brakemen quite a friendly fellow, and willing to talk.

"This rain will make matters worse," said he. "That tree was leaning against the bridge for all it was worth, and if it loosens any more it will carry the thing away clean."

"Isn't there danger of trains coming from the other way?"

"Not now. We've telegraphed to Chicago, and no train will leave till everything is in running order."

"When does the next train arrive behind us?"

"At 9.30 this morning."

We chatted for quite a while. Then there was a commotion on the platform, and we found that part of the wrecking gang had arrived on a hand-car.

They brought with them a great lot of tools, and soon a flat car with a hoisting machine was run out of a shed, and they were off.

By this time it was raining in torrents, and the station platform was deserted. Not caring to get wet, I again took my seat in the car, and presently fell asleep.

When I awoke I found it was six o'clock. The rain still fell steadily, without signs of abating.

I was decidedly hungry, and buttoning my coat up tightly about my neck, I sallied forth in search of a restaurant.

I found one within a block of the depot, and entering, I called for some coffee and muffins—first, however, assuring myself that my train was not likely to leave for fully an hour.

While busy with what the waiter had brought, I saw Mr. Allen Price enter. Luckily the table I sat at was full, and he was compelled to take a seat some distance from me.

Edward Stratemeyer

"Good morning, my young friend," said he, as he stopped for an instant in front of me.

I was surprised at his pleasant manner. He acted as if nothing had ever happened to bring up a coolness between us.

"Good morning," I replied briefly.

"Terrible rain, this, isn't it?"

"It is."

"My toothache's much better," he went on, "and I feel like myself once more. Funny I mistook your valise for mine, last night, wasn't it?"

"I don't know," I replied flatly.

I returned to my breakfast, and, seeing I would not converse further, the man passed on and sat down. But I felt that his eyes were on me, and instinctively I made up my mind to be on my guard.

As I was about to leave the place, several more passengers came in, and by what they said I learned that the train would not start for Chicago till noon, the bridge being so badly damaged that the road engineer would not let anything cross until it was propped up.

Not caring to go back to the train, I entered the waiting-room and took in all there was to be seen. At one end of the place was a news stand, and I walked up to this to look at the picture papers that were displayed.

I was deeply interested in a cartoon on the middle pages of an illustrated paper when I heard Mr. Price's voice asking for some Chicago daily, and then making inquiries as to where the telegraph once was located.

He did not see me, and I at once stepped out of sight behind him.

Having received his directions, Mr. Price sat down to write out his telegram. Evidently what he wrote did not satisfy him, for he tore up several slips of paper before he managed to prepare one that suited him.

Then he arose, and throwing the scraps in a wad on the floor, walked away.

Unobserved, I picked up the wad. Right or wrong, I was bound to see what it contained. Perhaps it might be of no earthly interest to me; on the other hand, it might contain much I would desire to know. Strange things had happened lately, and I was prepared for all sorts of surprises.

A number of the slips of paper were missing and the remainder were so crumpled that the pencil marks were nearly illegible.

At length I managed to fit one of the sheets together and then read these words:—

C. Hholtzmann>, Chicago:

Look out for a young man claiming to—

## CHAPTER XXIII

## IN CHICAGO

I had not been mistaken in my opinion of Mr. Allen Price. He was following me, and doing it with no good intention.

I concluded the man must be employed by Mr. Woodward. Perhaps I had seen him at some time in Darbyville, and so thought his face familiar.

I was glad that if he was a detective I was aware of the fact. I would now know how to trust him, and I made up my mind that if he got the best of me it would be my own fault.

One thing struck me quite forcibly. The merchant and John Stumpy both considered my proposed visit to Chris Holtzmann of importance. They would not have put themselves to the trouble and expense of hiring some one to follow me if this was not so. Though Mr. Aaron Woodward was rich, he was close, and did not spend an extra dollar except upon himself.

I was chagrined at the thought that Holtzmann would be prepared to receive me. I had hoped to come upon him unawares, and get into his confidence before he could realize what I was after.

I began to wonder when the telegram would reach Chicago. Perhaps something by good fortune might delay it.

Mr. Allen Price walked over to the telegraph office, and following him with my eyes I saw him pay for the message and then stroll away.

Hardly had he gone before I too stepped up to the counter.

"How long will it take to send a message to Chicago?" I asked of the clerk in charge.

"Probably till noon," was the reply. "The storm has crippled us, and we are having trouble with our lineman."

"It won't go before noon!" I repeated, and my heart gave a bound. "Are you sure?"

"Yes; perhaps even longer."

"How about the message that gentleman just handed in?"

"I told him I would send it as soon as possible,"

"Did you tell him it wouldn't go before noon?"

"No; he didn't ask," returned the clerk, coolly. He was evidently not going to let any business slip if he could help it.

"Is there any possible way I can get to Chicago before noon?" I went on.

The clerk shook his head. "I don't think there is," he replied.

"What is the nearest station on the other side of the bridge?"

Edward Stratemeyer

"Foley."

"And how far is that from Chicago?"

"Twelve miles."

"Thank you."

I walked away from the counter filled with a sudden resolve. I must reach Chicago before the telegram or Mr. Allen Price. If I did not, my trip to the city of the lakes would be a failure.

How was the thing to be accomplished? Walking out on the covered platform, out of sight of the man who was following me, I tried to solve the problem.

Smalleyville was a good ten miles from the misplaced bridge, and in a soaking rain such a distance was too far to walk. Perhaps I might get a carriage to take me to the spot. I supposed the cost would be several dollars, but decided not to stand on that amount.

I had about made up my mind to hunt up a livery stable, when some workingmen rolled up to the station on a hand-car.

"Where are you going?" I inquired of one of them.

"Down to the Foley bridge," was the reply,

"Will you take a passenger?" I went on quickly.

"You'll have to ask the boss."

The boss proved to be a jolly German.

"Vont ter haf a ride, does you!" he laughed.

"I'm not over particular about the ride," I explained. "I've got to get to Chicago as soon as possible, even if I have to walk."

"Vell, jump on, den."

I did so, and a moment later we were off. I was pretty confident that Mr. Allen Price had not witnessed my departure, and I hoped he would not find it out for some hours to come.

The rain had now slackened, so there was no further danger of getting soaked to the skin. There were four men on the car besides the boss, and seeing they were short a hand I took hold with a will.

Fortunately the grade was downward, and we had but little difficulty in sending the car on its way. At the end of half an hour the stream came in sight, and then as we slackened up I hopped off.

Down by the water's edge I found that the bridge had shifted fully six inches out of line with the roadbed. It was, however, in a pretty safe condition, and I had no difficulty in crossing to the other side.

Despite the storm a goodly number of men were assembled on the opposite bank, anxiously watching the efforts of the workmen. Among them I found a man, evidently a cabman, standing near a coupe, the horses of which were still smoking from a long run.

"Are you from Foley?" I asked, stepping up.

"No; just come all the way from Chicago," was the reply.

"Had to bring two men down that wanted to get to Smalleyville."

This was interesting news. Perhaps I could get the man to take me back with him. Of course he would take me if I hired him in the regular way, but if I did this, I was certain he would charge me a small fortune.

"I am going to Chicago," I said. "I just came from Smalleyville."

"That so? Want to hire my rig?"

"You charge too much," I returned. "A fellow like me can't afford luxuries."

"Take you there for two dollars. It's worth five—those two men gave me ten."

"What time will you land me in Chicago?"

"Where do you want to go?"

That question was a poser. I knew no more of the city of Chicago than I did of Paris or Pekin. Yet I did not wish to be set down on the outskirts, and not to show my ignorance I answered cautiously:—

"To the railroad depot."

"Have you the time now?"

"It is about seven o'clock."

"I'll be there by nine."

"All right. Land me there by that time, and I'll pay you the two dollars."

"It's a go. Jump in," he declared.

I did so. A moment later he gathered up the reins, and we went whirling down the road.

The ride was an easy one, and as we bowled along I had ample opportunity to ponder over my situation. I wondered what Mr. Allen Price would think when he discovered I was nowhere to be found. I could well imagine his chagrin, and I could not help smiling at the way I had outwitted him. I was not certain what sort of a man Chris Holtzmann would prove to be, and therefore it was utterly useless to plan a means of approaching him.

At length we reached the suburbs of Chicago, and rolled down one of the broad avenues. It was now clear and bright, and the clean broad street with its handsome houses pleased me very much.

In half an hour we reached the business portion of the city, and soon the coupe came to a halt and the driver opened the door.

"Here we are," said he.

I jumped to the ground and gazed around. Opposite was the railroad station, true enough, and beyond blocks and blocks of tall business buildings, which reminded me strongly of New York.

I paid the cabman the two dollars I had promised, and he drove off.

Edward Stratemeyer

In Chicago at last! I looked around. I was in the heart of a great city, knowing no one, and with no idea of where to go.

Yet my heart did not fail me. My mind was too full of the object of my quest to allow me to become faint-hearted. I was there for a purpose, and that purpose must be accomplished.

My clothes were still damp, but the sunshine was fast drying them. Near by was a bootblack's chair, and dropping into this, I had him polish my shoes and brush me up generally.

While he was performing the operation I questioned him concerning the streets and gained considerable information.

"Did you ever hear of a man by the name of Chris Holtzmann?" I asked.

"I dunno," was the slow reply. "What does he do?"

"I don't know what business he is in. He came from Brooklyn."

The bootblack shook his head.

"This city is a big place. There might be a dozen men by his name here. The street what you spoke about has lots of saloons and theatres on it. Maybe he's in that business."

"Maybe he is," I returned. "I must find out somehow."

"You can look him up in the directory. You'll find one over in the drug store on the corner."

"Thank you; I guess that's what I'll do," I replied.

When he had finished, I paid him ten cents for his work, and walked over to the place he had mentioned.

A polite clerk waited on me and pointed out the directory lying on a stand.

I looked it over carefully, and three minutes later walked out with Chris Holtzmann's new address in my pocket.

As I did so, I saw a stream of people issue from the depot. Some of them looked familiar. Was it possible that the train from Smalleyville had managed to come through, after all? It certainly looked like it.

I was not kept long in doubt. I crossed over to make sure, and an instant later found myself face to face with Allen Price!

# CHAPTER XXIV

## WHO MR. ALLEN PRICE WAS

I will not deny that I was considerably taken aback by my unexpected meeting with the man who had been following me. I had been firmly under the impression that he was still lolling around Smalleyville, waiting for a chance to continue his journey.

But if I was surprised, so was Mr. Allen Price. Every indication showed that he had not missed me at my departure, and that he was under the belief that I had been left behind.

He stopped short and gazed at me in blank astonishment.

"Why—why—where did you come from?" he stammered.

"From Smalleyville," I returned as coolly as I could. "And that's where you came from, too," I added.

"I didn't see you on the train," he went on, ignoring my last remark.

"I didn't come up by train."

"Maybe you walked," he went on, with some anxiety.

"Oh no; I rode in a carriage."

"Humph! It seems to me you must have been in a tremendous hurry."

"Perhaps I was."

"Why, you excite my curiosity. May I ask the cause of your sudden impatience?"

He put the question in an apparently careless fashion, but his sharp eyes betrayed his keen interest.

"You may."

"And what, was it?"

I looked at him for a moment in silence.

"I came to see a man."

"Ah! A friend? Perhaps he is seriously sick."

"I don't know if he is sick or not."

"And yet you hurried to see him?"

"Yes."

"Well, that—that is out of the ordinary." He hesitated for a moment. "Of course it is none of my business, but I am interested. Perhaps I know the party and can help you. May I ask his name?"

"It's the same man you telegraphed to," I returned.

Mr. Allen Price stopped short and nearly dropped his handbag. My unexpected reply had taken the "wind out of his sails."

"I telegraphed to?" he repeated.

"Exactly."

"But—but I telegraphed to no one."

"Yes, you did."

"Why, my dear young friend, you are mistaken."

"I'm not your dear friend," I returned with spirit. "You telegraphed to Chris Holtzmann to beware of me. Why did you do it?"

The man's face fell considerably, and he did not answer. I went on:—

"You are following me and trying to defeat the object of my trip to Chicago. But you shall not do it. You pretend to be an ordinary traveller, but you are nothing more than a spy sent on by Mr. Aaron Woodward to stop me. But I have found you out, and now you can go back to him and tell him that his little plan didn't work."

The man's brow grew black with anger. He was very angry, and I could see that it was with difficulty he kept his hands off me.

"Think you're smart, don't you?" he sneered.

"I was too smart for you."

"But you don't know it all," he went on. "You don't know it all—not by a jugful."

"I know enough to steer clear of you."

"Maybe you do."

The man evidently did not know what to say, and as a matter of fact, neither did I. I had told him some plain truths, and now I was anxious to get away from him and think out my future course of action.

"What's your idea of calling on Chris Holtzmann?" he went an after a long pause.

"That's my business."

"It won't do you any good."

"Perhaps it may."

"I know it won't," he replied in decided tones.

"What do you know about it?" I said sharply. "A moment ago you denied knowing anything about me. Now I've done with you, and I want you to leave me alone."

"You needn't get mad about it."

"I'll do as I please."

"No, you won't," he growled. "If you don't do as I want you to, I'll have you arrested."

This was strong language, and I hardly knew what to say in reply. Not that I was frightened by his threat, but what made the man take such a strong personal interest in the matter?

As I have said, I was almost certain I had seen the fellow before, though where and when was more than I could determine. Perhaps he was disguised.

"Perhaps you don't think I know who you are," I said quickly.

My words were a perfect shock to Mr. Allen Price. In spite of his bronzed face he turned pale.

"You know who I am? Why, I am as I tell you,—Allen Price," he faltered.

"Really," I replied, with assumed sarcasm.

"Yes, really."

"I know better," I returned boldly.

I was hardly prepared for what was to follow. The man caught me by the arm.

"Then what you know shall cost you dear," he cried. "I'm not to be outwitted by a country boy. Help! Police! Police!"

As he uttered his call for assistance he let drop his handbag and drew his purse from his pocket.

"I've got you, you young thief!" he cried, letting the purse fall to the sidewalk. "You didn't think to be caught as easily, did you? Help! Po—Oh, officer, I'm glad you've come!" the last to a policeman who had just hurried to the scene.

"What's the matter here?" demanded the minion of the law.

"I just caught this young fellow picking my pocket," exclaimed Mr. Allen. "Where's my pocketbook?"

"There's a pocketbook on the sidewalk," put in a man in the crowd that had quickly gathered.

"So it is." He picked it up. "You rascal! You thought to get away in fine style, didn't you?" he continued to me.

For a moment I was too stunned to speak. The un-looked-for turn of affairs took away my breath.

"I didn't pick his pocket," I burst out.

"Yes, you did."

"It isn't so. He's a swindler and is trying to get me into trouble."

"Here! here! none of that!" broke in the officer. "Tell me your story," he said to Mr. Allen Price.

"I was coming along looking in the shop windows," began my accuser, "when I felt a hand in my pocket. I turned quickly and just in time to catch this fellow trying to make off with my pocketbook."

"It is a falsehood, every word of it," I declared.

"Shut up!" said the officer, sternly. "Please go on."

"He is evidently a smart thief," continued Mr. Allen Price. "I must see if I have lost anything else."

Edward Stratemeyer

He began a pretended examination of his clothes. In the meantime the crowd began to grow larger and larger.

"We can't stay here all day," said the policeman, roughly. "What have you got to say to the charge?"

"I say it isn't true," I replied. "This man is a humbug. He is following me for a purpose, and is trying to get me into trouble."

"Ridiculous!" cried my accuser. "Why, I never heard of such a thing before!"

"That story won't wash," said the officer to me. "Do you make a charge?" he continued to Mr. Allen Price.

My accuser hesitated. "I will, if it is not necessary for me to go along," he said. "I am pressed for time. My name is Sylvester Manners. I am a partner in the Manners Clothing Company. You know the firm, I presume."

"Oh, yes, sir," replied the officer. He knew the Manners Clothing Company to be a rich concern.

"I will stop at the station house to-morrow morning and make a complaint," continued Mr. Allen Price. "Don't let the young rascal escape."

"No fear, sir. Come on!" the last to me.

"I've done no wrong. I want that man arrested!" I cried. "He is no more a merchant here in Chicago than I am. He—"

But the officer would not listen. He took a strong hold upon my collar and began to march me off. Mr. Allen Price walked beside us until we reached the corner.

"I will leave you here, officer," he said. "I'll be down in the morning, sure. As for you," he continued to me, "I trust you will soon see the error of your ways and try to mend them, and—" he continued in a whisper, as the officer's attention was distracted for a moment, "never try to outwit John Stumpy again!"

Edward Stratemeyer

# CHAPTER XXV

## AN EXCITING ADVENTURE

Mr. Allen Price and John Stumpy were one and the same person! For a moment so great was my surprise that I forgot I was under arrest, and walked on beside the officer without a protest.

Now that I knew the truth it was easy to trace the resemblance, and I blamed myself greatly for not having discovered it when we first met.

Of a certainty the man was bent upon frustrating my plans, partly for his own safety, and more so upon Mr. Aaron Woodward's account. No doubt the merchant was paying him well for his work, and John Stumpy intended to do all he could to crush me.

But I was not to be crushed. The forces brought against me only made my will stronger to go ahead. It was do or die, and that was all there was to it.

I could easily understand why John Stumpy wished to obtain possession of my handbag. In it he hoped to find the papers Mr. Woodward had lost and Nicholas Weaver's confession. I could not help but smile at the thought that, notwithstanding all I had said to the contrary, the two plotters still believed I had the lost documents.

One thing perplexed me. Why was my visit to Chris Holtzmann considered of such importance that every possible means was taken to prevent it? Did this man possess the entire key to the situation? And were they afraid he could be bought up or threatened into a confession? It looked so.

"You are not from Chicago, young fellow?" said the policeman who had me in charge.

"No; I'm from the East."

"Humph! Got taken in short, didn't you?"

"I'm not guilty of any crime," I returned, "and you'll find it out when it comes to the examination."

"I'll chance it," replied the officer, grimly.

"That man is a fraud. If you call on the Manners Clothing Company, you will find it so."

"That's not part of my duty. I'll take you to the station house, and you can tell the judge your story," replied the policeman.

Yet I could see by the way his brow contracted that my assertion had had its effect upon him. Probably had he given the matter proper thought in the first place, he would have compelled John Stumpy to accompany him.

Still, this did me no good. Here I was being taken to the jail while the man who should have been under arrest was free. I would probably have to remain in confinement until the following morning, and in the meantime John Stumpy could

Edward Stratemeyer

call on Chris Holtzmann and arrange plans to suit himself.

This would never do, as it would defeat the whole object of my trip West, and send me home to be laughed at by Mr. Aaron Woodward and Duncan.

"Can I ask for an examination at once?" I inquired.

"Maybe; if the judge is there."

"And if he isn't?"

"You'll have to wait till to-morrow morning. You see it isn't—Hello! thunder and lightning! what's that?"

As the officer uttered the exclamation there was a wild cry on the streets, and the next instant the crowds of people scattered in every direction.

And no wonder, for down the pavement came an infuriated bull, charging everybody and everything before him.

The animal had evidently broken away from a herd that was being driven to the stock-yards, and his nose, where the ring was fastened, was torn and covered with blood, and he breathed hard, as if he had run a great distance.

"It's a mad bull!" I cried. "Take care, or he'll horn both of us!"

My words of caution were unnecessary, for no sooner had the bull turned in our direction than the officer let go his hold upon me and fled into a doorway near at hand.

For an instant I was on the point of following him. Then came the sudden thought that now would be a good chance to escape.

To think was to act. No sooner had the policeman jumped into the doorway than I dodged through the crowd and hurried across the street. Reaching the opposite side, I ran into an alley. It was long and led directly into the back garden of a handsome stone mansion.

The garden was filled with beautiful flowers and plants, and in the centre a tiny fountain sent a thin spray into the air. At one side, under a small arbor, stood a garden bench, and on this sat a little girl playing with a number of dolls.

Her golden hair hung heavy over her shoulders, and she looked supremely happy. She greeted my entrance with a smile, and took me at once into her confidence.

"This is my new dolly," she explained, holding the article up.

"Is it?" I asked, hardly knowing what to say.

"Yes; papa bringed it home yesterday. Does oo like dollies?"

"Oh, yes, nice ones like that. You must have lots of fun. I—"

I did not finish the sentence. There was a noise in the alley, and the next instant the mad bull came crashing into the garden!

For a second I was too surprised to move or speak. The little girl uttered a piercing scream, and gathering her dolls in her arms huddled into a corner of the bench.

Why the animal had followed so closely behind me I could not tell, but once in the garden, it was plain to see he was bent upon doing considerable damage. He was more enraged than ever, and scattered the sodding about in every direction.

At first some red flowers attracted his attention, and he charged upon these with a fury that wrecked the entire flower-bed in which they were standing.

While the bull was at this work I partly recovered my senses, and then the first thought that came to my mind was the necessity of getting the little girl to a place of safety. Let the bull once get at her, and her life might pay the penalty. I was not many feet away from the little miss, and a few bounds took me to her side.

"Come, let me take you into the house," I said, and picked her up.

She made no reply, but continued to scream and clung to me with all the strength of her little arms.

There was a back piazza to the mansion five or six steps high. I knew that if we once reached this we would be safe, for no matter what the bull might do, he could not climb.

"Oh, Millie, my child!" came s voice from the house, and I saw a lady at one of the windows. "Oh, save her! Bring her here!" she cried, as she caught sight of the bull.

I uttered no reply, but sprang toward the steps.

But though I wasted no time, the bull was too quick for me. Springing over the flower-bed, he planted himself directly in my path.

It made my blood run cold to have him face me with that vicious look and those glaring eyes. One prod of those horns and all would be over.

"Oh, save Millie! Save my child!" The lady had opened the door and now came running out upon the piazza.

"I will if I can!" I returned. "Don't come down here. He'll tear you all to pieces!"

Even as I spoke the bull made a plunge for me. I darted to one side and sprang over to the edge of the piazza corner.

"Give her to me! Hand her up!" exclaimed the lady, as she rushed over, and as I held the little one on my shoulder, the lady drew her up and clasped the child, dolls and all, to her breast.

Hardly had I got rid of my charge than the bull came for me again. The trick I had played on him only served to increase his rage, and he snorted loudly.

I was in a bad fix. Between the piazza and the next-door fence was a distance of but ten feet, and behind me was the solid stone wall of the house. Escape on any side was impossible. Had I had time I might have climbed up to the piazza, but now this was not to be thought of, and another means of getting out of danger must be instantly devised.

"Oh, he will be killed!" cried the lady, in horror. "Help! help!"

I glanced around for some weapon with which to defend myself. I had nothing with me. Even my valise lay at the other end of the garden, where I had dropped it when the animal first made his appearance.

As I said, I looked around, and behind me found a heavy spade the gardener had at one time or another used for digging post holes. It was a strong and sharp implement, and

Edward Stratemeyer

I took it up with a good deal of satisfaction.

The bull charged on me with fury. As he did so, I took the spade and held it on a level with my waist, resting the butt end on the wall behind me.

The next instant there was a terrific crash that made me sick from head to foot. With all his force the bull had sprung forward, only to receive the sharp end of the spade straight between his eyes.

The blow was as if it had been delivered by an axe. It made a frightful cut, and the blood rushed forth in a torrent.

With a mad cry of pain the bull backed out. At first I thought he was going to charge me again, but evidently the blow was too much for him, for with several moans he turned, and with his head hanging down, he staggered across the garden to the alley and disappeared.

## CHAPTER XXVI

## SAMMY SIMPSON

I gave a sigh of relief when the bull was gone. The encounter with the mad animal had been no laughing matter. I had once heard of a man being gored to death by just such an infuriated creature, and I considered that I had had a narrow escape. I put my hand to my forehead and found the cold sweat standing out upon it. Taking my handkerchief, I mopped it away.

"Are you hurt?" inquired the lady, with great solicitation.

"No, ma'am," I replied. "But it was a close shave!"

"Indeed it was. And you saved my Millie's life! How can I thank you!"

"I didn't do so much. I guess she's scared a good bit."

"She hardly realized the danger, dear child. Did you, Millie, my pet?"

"The bad cow wanted to eat up my dollies!" exclaimed the little miss, with a grave shake of the head. "But oo helped me," she added, to me.

"I'm glad I was here," I returned.

"May I ask how you happened to come in?" continued the lady.

In a few words I told my story. I had hardly finished when the back door opened and a gentleman stepped out.

"What is the trouble here?" he asked anxiously. "I just heard that a mad bull had run into the garden."

"So he did, James; a savage monster indeed. This young man just beat him off and saved Millie's life."

"Hardly that," I put in modestly. I did not want more praise than I was justly entitled to receive.

"Indeed, but he did. See the spade covered with blood? Had he not hit the animal over the head with that, something dreadful would have happened."

"I didn't hit him exactly," I laughed. "I held it up and he ran against it," and once more I told my story.

"You have done us a great service, young man," said the gentleman when I had concluded. "I was once in the butcher business myself,—in fact, I am in it yet, but only in the export trade,—and I know full well how dangerous bulls can get. Had it not been for you my little girl might have been torn to pieces. One of her dolls is dressed in red, and this would have attracted the bull's immediate attention. I thank you deeply." He grasped my hand warmly. "May I ask your name?"

"Roger Strong, sir."

"My name is Harrison—James Harrison. You live here in Chicago, I suppose?"

"No, sir, I come from Darbyville, New Jersey."

"Darbyville?" He thought a moment. "I never heard of such a town."

"It is only a small place several miles from New York. I came to Chicago on business. I arrived about half an hour ago."

"Really? Your introduction into our city has been rather an exciting one."

"I've had other adventures fully as exciting in the past few days," I returned.

"Yes?" and Mr. Harrison eyed me curiously.

"Yes. Our train was delayed, I almost had my handbag stolen, and I've been arrested as a thief."

"And all in a half an hour?" The gentleman and his wife both looked incredulous.

"No, sir; since I've left home."

"I should like to hear your story—that is, if you care to tell it."

"I will tell you the whole thing if you care to listen," I returned, reflecting that my newly made friend might give me some material assistance in my quest.

"Then come into the house."

"I'd better shut the alley gate first," said I, and running down I did so, and picked up my handbag as well.

Mr. Harrison led the way inside. I could not help but note the rich furnishings of the place—the soft carpets, artistically papered walls, the costly pictures and bric-a-brac, all telling of wealth.

Mrs. Harrison and the little girl had disappeared up the stairs. Mr. Harrison ushered me into his library and motioned me to a seat.

I hardly knew how to begin my story. To show how John Stumpy had had me arrested, it would be necessary to go back to affairs at Darbyville, and this I hesitated about doing.

"If you have time I would like to tell you about my affairs before I started to come to Chicago," I said. "I would like your advice."

The gentleman looked at the clock resting upon the mantel shelf.

"I have an engagement at eleven o'clock," he returned. "Until then I am entirely at your service, and will be in the afternoon if you desire it. I'll promise to give you the best advice I can."

"Thank you. I am a stranger here, and most people won't pay much attention to a boy," I replied.

Then I told my story in full just as I have written it here. Mr. Harrison was deeply interested.

"It is a strange case," he said, when I had concluded. "These men must be thorough rascals, every one of them. Of course it yet remains to be seen what this Chris Holtzmann has to do with the affair. He may be made to give evidence for or against your father just as he is approached. I think I would be careful at the first meeting."

"I did not intend to let him know who I was."

"A good plan."

"But now if I venture on the street I may be arrested," I went on.

"It is not likely. Chicago is a big city, and unless the officer who arrested you before meets you, it is improbable that he can give an accurate enough description of you for others to identify you. Then again, having failed in his duty, he may not report the case at all."

"That's so; but if I do run across him—"

"Then send for me. Here is my card. If I can be of service to you, I shall be glad."

Mr. Harrison gave me minute directions how to reach Holtzmann's place. Then it was time for him to go, and we left the house together. I promised to call on him again before quitting Chicago.

It was with a lighter heart that I went on my way. In some manner I felt that I had at least one friend in the big city, to whom I could turn for advice and assistance.

Guided by the directions Mr. Harrison had given me, I had no difficulty in making my way in the direction of Chris Holtzmann's place of business or house, whatever it might prove to be.

Edward Stratemeyer

As I passed up one street and down another, I could not help but look about me with great curiosity. If Chicago was not New York, it was "next door" to it, and I could have easily spent the entire day in sightseeing.

But though my eyes were taking in all that was to be seen, my mind was busy speculating upon the future. What would Chris Holtzmann think of my visit, and what would be the result of our interview?

At length I turned down the street upon which his place was located. It was a wide and busy thoroughfare, lined with shops of all kinds. Saloons were numerous, and from several of them came the sounds of lively music.

"Can you tell me where Chris Holtzmann's place is?" I asked of a man on the corner.

"Holtzmann's? Sure! Down on the next corner."

"Thank you."

"Variety actor?" went on the man, curiously.

"Oh, no!" I laughed.

"Thought not. They're generally pretty tough—the ones Chris hires."

"Does he have a variety theatre?"

"That's what he calls it. But it's nothing but a concert hall with jugglers and tumblers thrown in."

I did not relish the idea of going into such a place, and I knew that my sister Kate and the Widow Canby would be horrified when they heard of it.

"What kind of a man is this Holtzmann?" I continued, seeing that the man I had accosted was inclined to talk.

"Oh, he's a good enough kind of a fellow if you know how to take him," was the reply. "He's a bit cranky if he's had a glass too much, but that don't happen often."

"Does he run the place himself?"

"What, tend bar and so?"

"Yes."

"Oh, no; he's too high-toned for that. He only bosses things. They say he's rich. Be came from the East some years ago with quite a little money, and he's been adding to it ever since."

"Then you know him quite well?"

"Worked for him two years. Then he up one day and declared I was robbing him. We had a big row, and I got out."

"Did he have you arrested?"

"Arrested? Not much. He knew better than to try such a game on me. When I was in his employ I kept my eyes and ears open, and I knew too much about his private affairs for him to push me, even if I had been guilty. Oh, Sammy Simpson knows a thing or two."

"That is your name?"

"Yes; Samuel A. Simpson. Generally called Sammy for short. I was his bookkeeper and corresponding clerk."

"Maybe you're just the man I want to see," I said. "Do you know anything about Mr. Holtzmann's private affairs in the East?"

"In Brooklyn?"

"Yes."

Sammy Simpson hesitated for a moment.

"Maybe I do," he replied, with a shrewd look in his eyes. "Is there anything to be made out of it?"

"I will pay you for whatever you do for me."

"Then I'm your huckleberry. Who are you and what do you want to know?"

# CHAPTER XXVII

## THE PALACE OF PLEASURE

Mr. Sammy Simpson was a character. He was tall and slim, certainly not less than fifty years of age, but with an evident desire to appear much younger. His face was cleanly shaven, and when he removed his hat to scratch his head I saw that he was nearly bald.

He was dressed in a light check suit and wore patent-leather shoes. I put him down as a dandy, but fond of drink, and that he proved to be.

"Whom do you work for now?" I asked.

"No one. To tell the truth, I'm down on my luck and I'm waiting for something to turn up."

"You say you worked for Holtzmann two years ago?"

"No, I said I worked for him two years. I only left last month."

"And he accused you of stealing?"

"Yes; but it was only to get rid of me because I knew too

Edward Stratemeyer

much of his private affairs."

"What do you know of his private affairs?"

Sammy Simpson rubbed his chin.

"Excuse me, but who am I talking to?" he asked abruptly.

"Never mind who I am. I am here to get all the information I can about Chris Holtzmann, and I'm willing to pay for it. Of course I'm not rich, but I've got a few dollars. If you can't help me I'll have to go elsewhere."

My plain speech startled Sammy Simpson.

"Hold up; don't get mad because I asked your name. You've a perfect right to keep it to yourself if you want to. Only make it sure to me that I'll get paid for what I tell and it will be all right."

I was perplexed. I had half a mind to mention Mr. Harrison's name, but if I did that, the man might expect altogether too much.

"I will promise you that you lose nothing," I said. "But we can't talk things over in the street. Tell me where I can meet you later on."

"Want to see Holtzmann first?"

"Yes."

"You won't get anything out of him, I'll wager you that."

"I don't expect to. I want to see what kind of a man he is."

"Well, you'll find me at 28 Hallock Street generally. If I'm not in, you can find out there where I've gone to."

"I'll remember it. In the meantime don't speak of this meeting to any one."

"Mum's the word," rejoined Sammy Simpson.

I went on my way deep in thought. I considered it a stroke of luck that I had fallen in with Chris Holtzmann's former clerk. No doubt the man knew much that would prove of value to me.

I doubted if this man was perfectly honest. I was satisfied that the concert-hall manager had had good grounds for discharging him. But it often "takes a rogue to catch a rogue," and I was willing to profit by any advantage that came to hand.

At length I reached the next corner. On it stood a splendid building of marble, having over the door in raised letters:—

CHRIS HOLTZMANN'S
PALACE OF PLEASURE.
Open all the Time. Admission Free!

For a moment I hesitated. Should I enter such a hole of iniquity?

Then came the thought of my mission; how I wished to clear the family name from the stain that rested upon it and free my father from imprisonment, and I went in.

I do not care to describe the scene that met my eyes. The magnificent decorations of the place were to my mind entirely out of keeping with its character. The foulness of a

Edward Stratemeyer

subcellar would have been more appropriate.

In the back, where a stage was located, were a number of small tables. I sat down at one of these and had a waiter bring me a glass of soda water.

"Is Mr. Holtzmann about?" I asked.

"Yes, sir. There he is over by the cigar counter. Shall I call him?"

"No."

I paid for my soda and sipped it leisurely. The place was about half full, and all attention was being paid to "Master Ardon, the Wonderful Boy Dancer," who was doing a clog on the stage.

Mr. Chris Holtzmann was very much the style of a man I had imagined him to be. He was short and stout, with a thick neck and a double chin. He was loudly dressed, including several seal rings and a heavy gold watch chain.

I calculated that he would be a hard man to approach, and now that I was face to face with him I hardly knew how to proceed.

At first I thought to ask him for a situation of some kind and thus get on speaking terms with him, but concluded that openness would pay best in the end, and so, rising, I approached him.

"Mr. Holtzmann, I believe?" I began.

"Yes," he said slowly, looking me over from head to foot.

"If you please I would like to have a talk with you," I went on.

"What is it?" and he turned his ear toward me.

"I have come all the way from Darbyville, New Jersey, to see you."

"What!" He started. "And what is your business with me, sir?" he went on sharply.

"I would like to see you in private," and I glanced at the clerk and several others who were staring at us.

"Come to my office," he returned, and led the way through a door at one side, into a handsomely furnished apartment facing the side street.

"Ross, you can post the letters," he said to a clerk who was writing at a desk. "Be back in half an hour."

It was a hint that we were to be left alone, and the clerk was not long in gathering up the letters that had been written, and leaving.

"I suppose Woodward sent you," began Chris Holtzmann, when we were seated.

This remark nearly took away my breath. I thought he would deny all knowledge of having ever known the merchant, and here he was mentioning the man at the very start.

I hardly knew how to reply, and he continued:—

"I've been expecting him for several days."

Edward Stratemeyer

"Well, you know there was an accident on the railroad," I began as coolly as I could. "The bridge shifted and the trains couldn't run."

"Yes, I heard of that." He paused for a moment. "What brought you?"

This was a home question. I plunged in like a swimmer into a deep stream.

"I came to get the papers relating to the Strong forgeries. You have all of them, I suppose."

I was surprised at my own boldness. So was my listener.

"Sh! not so loud," he exclaimed. "Who said I had the papers?"

"John Stumpy spoke about them to Mr. Woodward."

"He did, eh?" sneered Chris Holtzmann. "He had better keep his mouth shut. How does he know but what the papers were destroyed long ago?"

"I hope not," I replied earnestly.

"What does Woodward want of the papers?"

"I don't know exactly. The Strong family are going to have the case opened again, and he's afraid they may be dragged in."

"No one knows I have them but him, Stumpy—and you." He gave me a suspicious glance. "Who are—"

"The Strongs know," I put in hastily, thus cutting him off.

"What!" He jumped up from his chair. "Who was fool enough to tell them?"

"Nicholas Weaver left a dying statement—"

"The idiot! I always said he was a weak-minded fool!" cried Chris Holtzmann. "Who has this statement?"

"I don't know where it is now, but Carson Strong's son had it."

"Strong's son! Great Scott! Then Woodward's goose is cooked. I always told him he hadn't covered up his tracks."

"Yes, but he paid you pretty well for your share of the work," I returned. I was getting mixed. The deception could not be kept up much longer, and I wondered what would happen when the truth became known.

"Didn't pay me half of what I should have got. I helped him not only in Brooklyn, but here in Chicago as well. How would he have accounted for all his money if I hadn't had a rich aunt die and leave it to him?" Chris Holtzmann gave a short laugh. "I reckon that was a neat plan of mine."

"You ran a big risk."

"So we did—but it paid."

"And John Stumpy helped, too."

"He did in a way. But he drank too much to be of any great use. By the way, do you drink?"

As Holtzmann spoke he opened a closet at one side of the room, behind a screen, and brought forth a bottle of liquor and a pair of glasses.

"No, thank you," I replied.

"No? Have a cigar, then."

"Thank you; I don't smoke."

"What! Don't smoke or drink! That's queer. Wish I could say the same. Mighty expensive habits. What did you say your name was?"

At this instant there was a knock on the door, and Chris Holtzmann walked back of the screen and opened it.

"A man to see you, sir," I heard a voice say.

"Who is it?" asked Chris Holtzmann.

"Says his name is Aaron Woodward."

# CHAPTER XXVIII

## A DEAL FOR A THOUSAND DOLLARS

I was thunderstruck by the announcement that Mr. Aaron Woodward was waiting to come in. Had it been John Stumpy who was announced, I would not have been so much surprised. But Aaron Woodward! The chase after me was indeed getting hot.

Evidently the merchant was not satisfied to leave affairs in Chicago entirely in his confederate's hands. Either he did not trust Stumpy or else the matter was of too much importance.

I did not give these thoughts close attention at the time, but revolved them in my mind later. Just now I was trying to resolve what was best to do. Would it be advisable for me to remain or had I better get out?

To retire precipitately might not be "good form," but it might save me a deal of trouble. I had had one "round" with the merchant in his mansion in Darbyville, and I was not particularly anxious for another encounter. I was but a boy, and between the two men they might carry "too many guns" for me.

I looked around for some immediate means of escape. As I

have said, the office was located on the side street. Directly in front of the desk was a large window, opened to let in the fresh morning air. For me to think was to act. In less than a minute I was seated on the desk with my legs dangling over the window sill.

"Aaron Woodward!" repeated Chris Holtzmann, in evident surprise.

"Yes, sir, and he says he must see you at once."

"Did you hear that?" called out Holtzmann to me.

"Yes, I did," I returned as coolly as I could.

"Did you expect him?"

"No."

"Humph!"

Holtzmann made a movement as if to step into view, and I prepared to vanish from the scene. But he changed his mind and walked from the office.

I was in a quandary. To remain would place me in great peril, yet I was anxious to know the result of the meeting between the two men. They were the prime movers in my father's downfall, and nothing must be left undone to bring them to justice.

I resolved to remain, even if it were at the peril of my life. I was not an over-brave boy, but the thought of my father languishing in prison because of these men's misdeeds, nerved me to stay.

The closet door was still open, and that gave me a sudden idea.

As I jumped from the desk another idea struck me, and without any hesitation I scattered the papers on the floor and upset the ink-well.

Then I squeezed myself into the closet, crouching down into one corner, behind several canes and umbrellas.

I was not an instant too soon, for hardly had I settled myself than the door opened, and Chris Holtzmann reentered, followed by Mr. Aaron Woodward.

Both men were highly excited, and both uttered an exclamation when they saw the room was empty.

"He's gone!" cried Holtzmann.

"Gone?" repeated the merchant. "Get out, Holtzmann! He was never here."

"I say he was, less than two minutes ago."

"Well, where is he now?"

"I don't know. Ha! I see it! He has jumped through the windows. See how he has upset the ink and scattered the papers. It's as clear as day."

"Can you see anything of him outside?"

Chris Holtzmann leaned out of the window.

"No; he's up and around the corner long ago."

Edward Stratemeyer

"We must catch the rascal," went on Mr. Woodward, in a high voice. "He knows too much; he will ruin us both."

"Ruin us both?" sneered the proprietor of the Palace of Pleasure. "I don't see how he can ruin me."

"You're in it just as deep as I am—just as deep."

"Not a bit of it," returned Holtzmann, with spirit. "You are the only one who profited by the whole transaction, and you are the one to take the blame."

"See here, Chris, you're not going back on me in this way," exclaimed the merchant, in a tone of reproach.

"I'm not going back on you at all, Woody. But you can't use me as you used John Stumpy. It won't go down."

"Now don't get excited, Chris."

"I'm not excited. But I know a thing or two just as well as you do. If there is any exposure to take place, you must stand the brunt of it. You were a fool to let the boy get ahead of you."

"I didn't; it was Stumpy. He let the boy get hold of Nick Weaver's statement, and that started the thing. Then the boy stole some of my papers that were in my desk, and how much information he has now I don't know."

"All your own fault," responded Holtzmann, coolly. "Why don't you destroy all the evidence on hand?"

"Do you do that?" asked Mr. Woodward, furiously.

"I do when I think it isn't going to do me any more good,"

replied Holtzmann, evasively.

"Have you destroyed all the evidence in this matter?"

Holtzmann closed one eye. "I'm not so green as you take me to be," he replied impressively. "All my evidence against you is locked up in my safe."

"You intend to use it against me?" said the merchant.

"Only if it becomes necessary."

"And yet you pretend to be a friend of mine."

"I was until you cheated me out of my fair share of the spoils. But I am satisfied, and willing to let the whole matter rest."

"What will you take for the papers you hold?"

"Wouldn't sell them at any price. I'm not running my head into any trap."

"It will be all right."

"Maybe it will, but I'll run no risk," He paused a moment. "I'll tell you what I will do. Give me a thousand dollars and I'll let you see me burn them up.

I was intensely surprised at this proposition, more so, I believe, than was Mr. Woodward.

"A thousand dollars!" he exclaimed. "Chris, you're crazy."

"No, indeed. I know a thing or two. What do you suppose the Strongs would pay for them?"

"You don't mean to say you would play me false?" ejaculated the merchant, hoarsely.

"I mean to say I'd do anything to save myself if you got us into a hole. As far as I can see, you have allowed this boy to get the best of you at every turn."

"Humph! You needn't talk. You let him walk right into your confidence the first thing."

"Only when he told me all about your affairs."

"Well, let that drop. Can't you let me have the papers cheaper?"

"I said I wouldn't let you have the papers at all. I'll burn them up."

"Will you let me see them?"

Chris Holtzmann's brow contracted.

"What for?"

"Oh, I only want to make sure of what you've got.

"Will you pay the price?"

"Make them cheaper."

"No."

"I'll take them."

"You mean have them burnt up."

"Yes. But I must examine them first."

"I'm willing. And I must have my check before they go into the fire."

"You are very suspicious, Chris, very suspicious."

"No more so than you, Woody. I wasn't born yesterday."

"Well, let's have the papers and I'll write out the check. But it must be understood that you give no more information to the boy."

"Give him information!" cried Holtzmann. "Let him show his face here again and I'll break every bone in his body," he added grimly.

This was certainly an interesting bit of news. I made up my mind that to be seen would render matters decidedly warm for me.

But I was even more interested over the fact that the two men intended to burn up part of the evidence that might clear my father's name. Such a thing must not happen. I must use every means in my power to prevent it.

Yet what was to be done? If the documents were produced at once, how could I save them from destruction?

A bold dash for them seemed the only way. Once snatched from Holtzmann's or Aaron Woodward's hands, and escape through the window or the door would be difficult, but not impossible.

Yet while I was revolving these thoughts over in my mind the same thing evidently suggested itself to the proprietor of the Palace of Pleasure.

"Wait till I lock the door," he said. "We don't want to be interrupted."

"No indeed," returned Mr. Woodward; "interruptions don't pay."

"And I'll close the window, too," went on Holtzmann; "it's cool enough without having it open."

"So it is."

So the window and the door were both closed and fastened. I was chagrined, but could do nothing.

A moment later I heard Chris Holtzmann at his safe, and then the rattle of something on his desk.

"The papers are in this tin box," he said. "I placed them there over six months ago."

He opened the box, and I heard a rustling of documents.

"Why—why—what does this mean!" he ejaculated. "They are not here!"

"What!" cried Mr. Aaron Woodward, aghast.

"The papers are not here!" Holtzmann hurried over to his safe and began a hasty search. "As sure as you're born, Woody, they have been stolen!"

"It's that boy," exclaimed the merchant. "He's a wizard of a sly one. He has stolen them, and we are lost!"

# CHAPTER XXIX

## THE PRECIOUS PAPERS

I was not as much surprised over the situation as were the two men. I could put two and two together as quickly as any one, and I knew exactly where the papers were to be found.

Sammy Simpson, of 28 Hallock Street, was the thief. He had intimated that he had evidence against Chris Holtzmann, and these papers were that evidence.

This being so, there was no further use for my remaining in my cramped position in the closet, and I longed for a chance for escape. It was not long in coming.

"I don't see how that boy managed it," said Holtzmann. "He was alone only a few minutes."

"Never mind. He's as smart as a steel trap. Was the safe door open?"

"Yes. My clerk left it open. He is a new one and rather careless. What's to be done?"

"I'm going after the rascal," cried Aaron Woodward.

Edward Stratemeyer

"You'd have a fine time finding him here in Chicago."

"I must find him. Most likely when he discovers how valuable the papers are he'll be off at once for home with them. I can intercept him at the depot."

"That's an idea, if you can locate the right depot."

"I'll be off at once," went on Mr. Woodward.

"I'll go with you," returned Chris Holtzmann, and three minutes later the two men quitted the office, locking the door after them.

I waited several minutes to make sure they were not returning, and then emerged from my hiding-place.

I was stiff in every joint and nearly stifled from the hot air in the closet. But at present I gave these personal matters scant attention, my mind being bent upon escape.

Even if the door had been unlocked, I would not have chosen it as a means of egress. It led into the main hall of the Palace of Pleasure, and here I might meet some one to bar my escape.

The window was close at hand, and I threw it open. The noise I made did not frighten me, for in the main hall a loud orchestra was drowning out every other sound.

I looked out and saw a number of people walking up and down the street. No one appeared to be watching me, and waiting a favorable opportunity, I slid out of the window to the sidewalk below.

With my ever present handbag beside me I hurried down the

side street as fast as my feet would carry me. The neighborhood of the Palace of Pleasure was dangerous for me, and I wished to get away from it as quickly as possible.

After travelling several blocks I slackened my pace and dropped into a rapid walk. Coming to a fruit-stand, I invested in a couple of bananas, and then asked its proprietor where Hallock Street was.

"Sure an' it's the first street beyant the cable road," was the reply.

"And where is the cable road?" I queried.

"Two squares that way, sor," and the woman pointed it out.

I thanked her and hurried on. When I reached the street, I found the numbers ran in the three hundreds, and I had quite a walk to the southward to reach No. 28.

At length I stood in front of the house. It was a common-looking affair, and the vicinity was not one to be chosen by fastidious people. The street, sidewalks, and doorways all looked dirty and neglected. I concluded that since being discharged Sammy Simpson had come down in the world.

"Does Mr. Simpson live here?" I asked of a slip of a girl who sat on the stoop, nursing a ragged doll.

"Yes, sir; on the third floor in the front," she replied.

I climbed up the creaky stairs two flights, and rapped on the door.

"Come," said a voice, and I entered. The room was the barest kind of a kitchen. By the open window sat a thin, pale woman, holding a child.

"Does Mr. Samuel Simpson live here?" I asked.

"Yes, sir, but he's not in now," she returned. "Can I do anything for you?"

"I guess not."

"I hope—I hope there is nothing wrong," she went on falteringly.

"Wrong?" I queried. I did not quite understand her.

"Yes, sir."

"Not exactly. What makes you think so?"

"Because he drinks so," she replied.

"I wish to get some information from him; that is all," I returned.

As I concluded a heavy step sounded in the hall, and an instant later Sammy Simpson appeared. He had evidently been imbibing freely, for his voice was thick and his sentences muddled.

"Hello!" he cried. "You here already, eh! What brought you? Want to find out all about Chris Holtzmann?"

"Yes."

"Thought so. Saw it in your eye. Yes, sir, your optic betrayed you. Sit down. Mag, give Mr. What's-his-name a chair. I'll sit down myself." And he sank heavily down on a low bench, threw one leg over the other, and clasped his hands on his knee.

"I want to see those documents you took from Mr. Holtzmann's safe," I began boldly.

He started slightly and stared at me.

"Who said I took any document out of his safe?"

"Didn't you say so? I mean the ones relating to Holtzmann's affairs in Brooklyn."

"Well, yes, I did."

"I want to see them."

"Again I ask, what is there in it?" he exclaimed dramatically.

"If they really prove of value to me, I will pay you well for all your trouble," I replied.

"Is that straight?" he asked thickly.

"It is," I replied, and, I may as well add, I was thoroughly disgusted with the man.

"Then I'm yours truly, and no mistake. Excuse me till I get them."

Be rose unsteadily and left the room. Hardly had he gone before his wife hurried to my side.

"Oh, sir, I hope you are not getting him into trouble?" she cried. "He is a good man when he is sober; indeed he is,"

"I am not going to harm him, madam. A great wrong has been done, and I only want your husband to assist me in righting it. He has papers that can do it."

"You are telling me the truth?" she questioned earnestly.

"Yes, ma'am."

"I think I can trust you," she said slowly. "You look honest. And these papers—ought you to have them?"

"Yes. If your husband does not give them up, he will certainly get into great trouble."

"You are young, and you don't look as if you would lie. If Sam has the papers, he shall give them to you. He's coming now."

"Here's all the evidence in the case," said Sammy Simpson, on returning. He held a thick and long envelope. "What's the value to you?"

"I can tell better after I have examined them," I returned.

"Will you give them back if I let you see them?"

"Yes."

He handed the precious papers to me and then sat down.

Oh, how eagerly I grasped the envelope! How much of importance it might contain for me!

There were three letters and four legal papers. Like Nicholas Weaver's statement, all were badly written, and I had a hard job to decipher even a portion of the manuscript.

Yet I made out enough to learn that Aaron Woodward was the forger of the notes and checks that had sent my father to prison, and that the death of a relative in Chicago was only a pretence. The work had been done in Brooklyn through that branch of Holland & Mack's establishment. Chris Holtzmann had helped in the scheme, and John Stumpy had presented one of the checks, for which service he had received six hundred dollars. This much was clear to me. But two other points still remained dark.

One was of a certain Ferguson connected with the scheme, who seemed to be intimate with my father. He was probably the man my father had mentioned when we had visited him at the prison. His connection with the affair was far from clear.

The other dark point in the case was concerning Agatha Mitts, of 648 Vannack Avenue, Brooklyn. She was a boarding-mistress, and the three or four men had stopped at her house. But how much she knew of their doings I could not tell.

"Well, what do you think?" muttered Sammy Simpson. "Mighty important, I'll be bound."

"Not so very important," I returned, as coolly as I could. "They will be if I can get hold of other papers to use with them."

"Exactly, sir; just as I always said. Well, you can get them easily enough, no doubt."

"I don't know about that," I said doubtfully.

"No trouble at all. Come, what will you give?"

Edward Stratemeyer

"Five dollars."

"Ha! ha! They're worth a million." He blinked hard at me. "Say, you're a friend of mine, a good boy. Meg, shall I give them to him?"

"You ought to do what's right, Sam," replied his wife, severely.

"So I ought. You're a good woman; big improvement on a chap like me. Say, young man, give my lady ten dollars, keep the papers, and clear out. I'm drunk, and when Sammy Simpson's drunk he's a fool."

I handed over the money without a word. Perhaps I was taking advantage of the man's present state, but I considered I was doing things for the best.

A minute later, with the precious papers in my pocket, I left.

# CHAPTER XXX

## THE TRAIN FOR NEW YORK

Down in the street I hesitated as to where to go next. I felt that the case on hand was getting too complicated for me, and that I needed assistance.

I did not relish calling on the police for help. They were probably on the watch for me, and even if not, they would deem me only a boy, and give me scant attention.

My mind reverted to the adventure earlier in the day, and I remembered Mr. Harrison's kind offer. I had done his little daughter a good turn, and I was positive the gentleman would assist me to the best of his ability.

I decided to call on him at once. I had his address still in my pocket, and though I was quite tired, I hurried along at a rapid rate.

On the way I revolved in my mind all that had occurred within the past two hours, and by the time I reached Mr. Harrison's place I had the matter in such shape that I could tell a clear, straightforward story.

I found the gentleman in, and pleased at my return.

Edward Stratemeyer

"I was afraid you had gotten into more difficulties," he explained, with a smile.

"So I did but I got out of them again," I replied.

Sitting down, I gave him the particulars of my visit to Chris Holtzmann and to Sammy Simpson, and handed over the documents for inspection. Mr. Harrison was deeply interested, and examined the papers with great care. It took him nearly an hour to do so, and then he plied me with numerous questions.

"Do you know what my advice is?" he asked, at length.

"No, sir."

"I advise you to have both Holtzmann and Woodward arrested at once. They are thorough rascals, and your father is the innocent victim of their cupidity."

"But how can I do that? No one knows me here in Chicago."

"Hold up, you make a mistake. I know you."

"Yes, but you don't know anything about me," I began.

"I know you to be a brave fellow, and brave people are generally honest. Besides, your face speaks for itself."

"You are very kind."

"I have not forgotten the debt I owe you, and whatever I do for you will never fully repay it."

"And you advise me—"

"To put the case in the hands of the police without delay. Come, I will go with you. Perhaps this Holtzmann may be frightened into a confession."

"I trust so. It will save a good deal of trouble."

"Woodward can be taken into custody as soon as the necessary papers are made out," concluded. Mr. Harrison.

An instant later we were on the way. I wondered what had become of John Stumpy. It was strange that he had not turned up at the Palace of Pleasure. Perhaps Mr. Aaron Woodward had intercepted him and either scared or bought him off.

The fellow held much evidence that I wished to obtain, for every letter or paper against Mr. Woodward would make my father's case so much stronger, and I determined with all my heart that when once brought to trial there should be no failure to punish the guilty, so that the innocent might be acquitted.

At the police station we found the sergeant in charge. Mr. Harrison was well known in the locality, and his presence gained at once for us a private audience.

The officer of the law gave the case his closest attention, and asked me even more questions than had been put to me before.

"I remember reading of this affair in the court records," he said. "Judge Fowler and I were saying what a peculiar case it was. Chris Holtzmann claims to keep a first-class resort, and I would hardly dare to proceed against him were it not for these papers, and you, Mr. Harrison."

"You will arrest him at once?" questioned the gentleman.

"If you say so."

"I do, most assuredly."

"You are interested in the case?" queried the sergeant, as he prepared to leave.

"Only on this young man's account. He saved my little daughter from a horrible death this morning."

"Indeed? How so?"

"There was a mad bull broke into my back garden from the street, and was about to gore her, when this young man, who had been driven into the garden in the first place, came between and drove the bull out."

"Oh, I heard of that bull."

"What became of him?" I put in curiously.

"He was killed by a couple of officers on the next block. He was nearly dead before they shot him, having received a terrible cut between the eyes."

"Given by this young man," explained Mr. Harrison.

"You don't mean it!" cried the officer, in admiration. "Phew! but you must be strong!"

"It was more by good luck than strength," I returned modestly.

"Nonsense!" said Mr. Harrison. "My wife witnessed the

whole occurrence, and she says it was pure bravery."

Five minutes later a cab was called, and we all got in. I was not sorry to ride, for my long tramp from one place to another on the stone pavement had made me footsore. I did not mind walking, but the Darbyville roads were softer than those of Chicago.

It did not take long to reach the Palace of Pleasure.

"Just wait in the cab for a minute or two," said the sergeant to me. "If he sees you first, he may make a scene."

"Most likely he's gone out," I returned.

The sergeant and Mr. Harrison left the carriage and entered the building.

I awaited their return impatiently. Would they get their man? And would Mr. Aaron Woodward be along?

Five—ten minutes dragged slowly by. Then the two returned.

"He's not in the place, and no one knows where he has gone," said the officer.

"He can't be far off," I replied. "No doubt he and Mr. Woodward have gone off to look for me."

"And where?" put in Mr. Harrison. I thought a moment.

"The depot!" I exclaimed. "He spoke about looking for me there."

"Then we'll be off at once," returned the sergeant.

As he spoke, a familiar figure came shambling around the corner. It was Sammy Simpson.

"Hello, you!" he cried, on catching sight of me. "I want those papers back."

"Why do you want them back?" I asked.

"You didn't pay the value of 'em, didn't pay enough," he hiccoughed.

"I paid all I agreed to."

"Can't say anything about that. But 'tain't enough." He glared at me. "Holtzmann said he'd pay me a hundred dollars. Yes, sir, ten times as much as you."

"When de you see Holtzmann?" I cried, in great interest.

"Saw him about half an hour ago. He came to see me—came to see Sammy Simpson—climbed the stairs to my abode. Wanted the papers—said I must have 'em. Went wild with rage when I let slip you had 'em. So did the other gent."

"Who? Mr. Woodward?"

"That's the identical name. Yes, sir—the correct handle. And they wanted the papers. Offered a hundred dollars for 'em. Think of it. Here's the ten dollars—give 'em back."

Had Sammy Simpson been sober he would not have made such a simple proposition.

"No, sir," I replied decidedly. "A bargain's a bargain. I've got the papers, and I intend to keep them."

"No, you don't."

"What's that?" broke in the sergeant of police.

"I want those papers."

"Do you know who I am?"

"No, and don't care."

"I am sergeant of police, and I want you to behave yourself, or I'll run you in," was the decided reply.

At the mention of an officer Sammy Simpson grew pale.

"No, no, don't do that. I've never been arrested in my life."

"The papers are in the hands of the proper parties," went on the sergeant.

"Then I can't have 'em back?"

"No; and the less you have to do with the whole matter, the better off you'll be. Where has Holtzmann gone?"

"To Brooklyn."

I was astonished. To Brooklyn, and so soon!

"You are sure?" I queried.

"Yes; he and the other gent intended to take the first train."

Here was indeed news. This sudden and unexpected departure must portend something of importance.

"We must catch them!" I exclaimed.

"Do you know anything about the trains?" asked Mr. Harrison.

"No."

"Jump in, and we'll be off to the depot," said the sergeant.

In an instant we had started, leaving Sammy Simpson standing in the middle of the pavement too astonished to speak. It was the last I ever saw of the man.

We made the driver urge his horse at the top of his speed. I calculated that the pair would take the same line that had brought me to Chicago.

I was not mistaken; for when we reached the depot a few questions put by the sergeant revealed the fact that the two men had purchased tickets for New York but a minute before.

"And when does the train leave?" I asked.

"Her time's up now."

At that instant a bell rang.

"There's the bell."

"We must catch her," I cried, and ran though the gate and on to the platform.

But the train was already moving. I tried to catch her, but failed; and a minute later the cars rolled out of sight.

Mr. Aaron Woodward and Chris Holtzmann had escaped me.

What was to be done next?

# CHAPTER XXXI

## IN THE METROPOLIS

I was thoroughly chagrined when I stood on the platform and saw the train roll away. Now that I had Mr. Harrison and the sergeant of police with me I had fondly hoped to capture the two men, even if it was at the last minute.

But now that chance was gone, and as I turned back to my two companions I felt utterly nonplussed.

One thing was perfectly clear in my mind. The two men had gone to Brooklyn to see Mrs. Agatha Mitts. No doubt they thought that now I had the papers Sammy Simpson had stolen in my possession I would follow up the train of evidence by calling on the woman—a thing I most likely would have done. They intended to head me off, and by this means break down my case against them at its last stage.

Yet though I was disappointed I was not disheartened. I was fighting for honor and intended to keep on until not a single thing remained to do. My evidence against Woodward and Holtzmann was gradually accumulating, and sooner or later it must bring them to the bar of justice.

"Well, they're gone," I exclaimed, as I joined the others.

"That is, if they were on that train."

"We'll ask the gateman and make sure," said the sergeant.

This was done, and we soon learned that beyond a doubt Mr. Woodward and Chris Holtzmann had been among the departed passengers.

"My work in Chicago is at an end," remarked the sergeant, as we stood in the waiting-room discussing the situation.

"And so is mine," I replied. "I've got the papers, and now the two men are gone, there is no use of my remaining."

"What do you intend to do?" asked Mr. Harrison.

"Follow them to Brooklyn."

"To Brooklyn? It's a good distance."

"I can't help it; I must go. As for the distance, it is not many miles from my home."

Mr. Harrison mused for a moment.

"I have an idea of going along with you," he said at length.

"Going along with me!" I repeated, astonished by his offer.

"Yes; I intended to take a trip to New York, on special business next week, but I can go to-day instead. You no doubt need help, and I want to give it to you."

"You are very kind," I replied.

"I would like to see you and your family get your rights," he

Edward Stratemeyer

went on. "I wonder when the next train leaves."

"I'll find out at the ticket office," I replied.

I walked over to the box, and at the window learned that the next train would not start for two hours and a half.

"That will give me time to go home, pack my valise, and arrange my affairs," said Mr. Harrison. "Come, you can go with me, and we can dine together."

"Thank you," was my answer.

"And you, sergeant. I will be pleased to have you, too," continued Mr. Harrison, turning to the officer.

"You're kind, Mr. Harrison, but duty calls me elsewhere. I'll have to return to the station. But you've forgotten one thing."

"What?"

"That you can telegraph to New York and have the two men arrested as soon as they arrive."

"That's so! What do you say, Strong?"

I thought for a moment. It would be the simplest way to do, but would it be the best?

"Don't you think we had better let them go ahead?" I returned. "We know exactly where they are going, and by following them up may gain some additional information."

"I don't know but what you are right," replied Mr. Harrison.

"Then, in that case, my duty here is at an end," said the sergeant.

"I'm very much obliged for the trouble you've taken. Are there any charges to pay?"

"None at all. Good day. Hope you will meet with success in the future."

"Thank you. If we do, I'll write you."

"Now we'll jump into a cab at once," said Mr. Harrison, when we were alone.

A minute later we were whirling along in the direction of his mansion.

"I hope you are not taking too much trouble on my account," I observed.

"I don't consider it too much," he replied. "Even if I had no business of my own to call me to New York I would go along if I thought I would be of service to you. You saved my little girl's life, and that debt, as I have told you before, I can never repay you."

We soon reached Mr. Harrison's mansion. Of course Mrs. Harrison was surprised at her husband's sudden determination, but when the situation was explained to her, she urged him to do his best for me.

The dinner served was the most elegant I had ever eaten, and despite the excited state of mind I was in, I did ample justice to it. Little Millie was present, and during the progress of the meal we became great friends.

Edward Stratemeyer

But all good things must come to an end, and an hour later, each with his handbag, we entered the cab and were off.

On the way we stopped at Mr. Harrison's office, where that gentleman left directions concerning things to be done during his absence. Evidently he was a thorough business man, and I could not help but wonder what he was worth when I saw him place several hundred dollars in bills in his pocketbook.

Arriving at the depot, we found we had just five minutes to spare. This Mr. Harrison spent in the purchase of a ticket for himself—I had mine—and in getting parlor-car seats for both of us.

It was a novelty to me to have such a soft chair to sit in, and I thoroughly enjoyed it.

As we rode along, my kind friend questioned me closely about myself, and I ended by giving him my entire history.

"You've had rather a hard row to hoe, and no mistake," he said. "It is a dreadful thing to have one's family honor assailed. Many a man has broken down completely under it."

"It is so with my father," I replied. "He used to be as bright as any one, but now he doesn't have much hope of any kind left."

In the evening another surprise awaited me. Instead of remaining in the comfortable chair, Mr. Harrison bade me follow him to the sleeping-car, and I was assigned as soft a bed as I had ever occupied. I slept "like a top," resolved to get the full value of so elegant an accommodation. When I awoke, it was broad daylight.

I climbed down from my bed and made my toilet leisurely. When I had finished, Mr. Harrison appeared, and together we had breakfast, and, five hours later, dinner.

It was six o'clock in the evening when we rolled into the station at Jersey City, and alighted. I was a little stiff from the long ride, but not near as much so as I would have been had I travelled in the ordinary cars.

"We'll cross the ferry at once," said Mr. Harrison. "The sooner we get to New York, the better."

"And the sooner we get to Brooklyn, the better," I added. "Do you think it will be advisable for me to hunt up Mrs. Agatha Mitts to-night?"

"I think it would. Even if you don't call on her, you can find out about her and see how the land lies. We will find a hotel to stop at first."

We were soon in New York and on our way up Broadway. Opposite the post-office we found an elegant hotel, where Mr. Harrison hired a room for himself.

He insisted on my having supper with him. Then leaving our handbags in his room, we started for the Fulton Street ferry to Brooklyn.

It was now growing dark, and the streets were filled with people hurrying homeward. I tried to keep as close to Mr. Harrison as possible, but something in a window attracted my attention, and when I looked around he was gone.

I supposed he had gone on ahead and hurried to catch him. But in this I was mistaken, for in no direction could I catch sight of the gentleman.

Edward Stratemeyer

Deeply concerned, I stood on the corner of a narrow street or alley, undecided what to do. Should I go on to Brooklyn or retrace my steps to the hotel?

I had about made up my mind to go on, when a disturbance down the alley attracted my attention.

Straining my eyes in the semi-darkness, I discovered several rough-looking young fellows in a group.

"Give it to him, Bandy; hit him over the head!" I heard one of them exclaim.

"Fair share of plunder, Mickey," cried another.

And then I saw a helpless young man in their midst, who was being beaten and no doubt robbed.

I did not give thought to the great risk I ran, but hurried at once to the scene.

"What are you doing here?" I asked.

"Help me! help me!" called out the young man, in a beseeching voice.

I stared at him in amazement. And no wonder. The young man was Duncan Woodward.

# CHAPTER XXXII

## A NIGHT AT THE HOTEL

"Duncan Woodward!" I exclaimed. "Is it possible?"

He gave me a quick look of wonder. "Roger Strong!" he gasped. Oh, save me, Roger! These rowdies want to kill me!"

Even as he spoke he received a cruel blow in the side.

"I'll help you all I can," I replied promptly.

I knew it would be a waste of words to try to argue with the gang of toughs, so I simply went at them in a physical way.

I hit out right and left with all my might, and as quickly as I could, repeated the blows.

The suddenness of my attack disconcerted the three footpads, and when Duncan recovered sufficiently to lend a hand, one of them took to his heels and disappeared up the alley.

The two remaining ones stood their ground, and called on their companions to come back and bring "Noxy an' de rest."

I received a blow in the shoulder that nearly threw me over

Edward Stratemeyer

on my back. But I straightened up, and in return gave my assailant a hard one in the nose that drew blood.

"Duncan, you clear out to the street," I whispered. "I'll come after."

The young man followed my advice, first, however, stopping to pick up several things he had dropped or that had been taken from him.

When he was twenty or thirty feet away I started after him. As I did so, I noticed he had left a large note-book lying on the ground. I took it up, and hurried on. For a moment more we were safe upon the street again, and the two toughs slunk away up the alley.

Then, for the first time, I noted something about Duncan that I thought shameful beyond words.

He had been drinking heavily. The smell of liquor was in his breath, and it was with difficulty that he kept from staggering.

"You're my best, friend," he mumbled. "My enemy and my friend."

"What are you doing in New York, Duncan?" I asked.

"Come on important business, Roger. Say, take me to the hotel, will you? That's a good fellow."

"Where are you staying?"

"Staying? Nowhere."

"Then why don't you take the train to Newville and

go home?"

"Can't do that."

"Why not?"

"The old gent would kill me. He says I spend too much money. Well, maybe I do."

"You've bean drinking, Duncan."

"So I have, Roger. Take me to a hotel."

"Will you promise to go to bed and not to drink any more if I do?"

"Yes. I've had enough."

"Then brace up and come with me."

Not without a good deal of difficulty did I manage to make him walk several blocks to a good though not stylish hotel. Here I took him into the office and explained the situation to the clerk in charge, who promptly assigned us to a room on the third floor.

The charge was three dollars, which Duncan with some difficulty managed to pay; and then we took the elevator to the third floor.

The room was a good one, with a soft bed. No sooner did Duncan reach it than he sank down, and in five minutes he was fast asleep.

I was in a quandary as to what to do. I did not care to leave him in his present state, and at the same time I was anxious to find Mr. Harrison and visit Mrs. Agatha Mitts in Brooklyn.

I wondered if my kind friend from Chicago had gone on without me, until I suddenly remembered that the Brooklyn address was in my pocket, and that he probably did not remember the street and number.

This being the case, he had no doubt returned to the hotel and was awaiting me.

I looked at Duncan, and made up my mind that he would sleep several hours, if not longer, without awaking.

Making him as comfortable as possible on the bed, I left the room, locking the door behind me.

Down in the office I explained the situation to the clerk when I left the key, and he promised to attend to matters if anything unusual happened.

I was not very well acquainted with New York City, and in trying to find my way to the hotel at which Mr. Harrison was stopping, I nearly lost my way.

But several inquiries, made here and there, set me right, and at length I reached the large, open corridor.

As I was about to step into the office, a well-known voice hailed me.

"Well, here you are at last." Of course it was Mr. Harrison.

"Yes, sir."

"Did I lose you, or vice versa?" he went on.

"I don't know. I'm sure it wasn't intentional, anyway."

"Have you been over to Brooklyn?" he continued curiously.

"No, sir."

"I thought you had; it is so long since we parted."

"I've had quite an adventure in the meantime."

"Indeed? You didn't meet Chris Holtzmann or this Aaron Woodward, did you?"

"I met Mr. Woodward's son," I replied, and in a brief way I related my adventures. Mr. Harrison listened with deep interest.

"It is too bad that the son has started in such a wrong path," he said. "I trust it teaches him a lesson to let liquor alone. What do you intend to do now?"

"I suppose I had better go back and stay all night with him. It is now too late to go to Brooklyn."

"I think you are right. I can call for you at, say, eight o'clock in the morning."

This was agreed upon, and as it was then after nine o'clock, I hurried back to Duncan at once. I found him still sleeping, and I did not disturb him. There was a lounge in the room, and throwing off my coat, vest, and shoes, I made my bed upon this.

For once I found it difficult to sleep. It seemed to me that my adventures must soon come to an end. Was it the fore-shadowing of coming events that disturbed me? I could not tell. I wondered how all were at home; my sister Kate, Uncle Enos, and the Widow Canby, and I prayed God that I might be permitted to bring good news to them.

About midnight I fell into a light doze. Half an hour later I awoke with a start. Some one was talking in the room. Sitting up, I listened intently. It was Duncan, muttering in his sleep.

"Lift the spring, Pultzer," he said in a whisper. "Hist! don't make so much noise, the old gent may hear you." He paused for a moment. "There wasn't any money. But I've got the papers, yes, I've got the papers, and when I find out their true value the old gent shall pay me to keep quiet."

I could not help but start at Duncan's words. Like a flash of lightning came the revelation to me. He had entered his father's library and taken the papers which Mr. Woodward had accused me of stealing.

It was as clear as day. It explained why Pultzer, accompanied by another, who must have been of the party, had been out so late the night of the robbery. They had helped Duncan in his nefarious work, hoping they would be rewarded by the finding of a sum of money. Evidently the Models were a bad set, and I was thoroughly glad Dick Blair had turned his back upon them.

I waited with bated breath for Duncan to continue his speaking, but was disappointed. He turned over on his side and dreamed on, without a word.

At length I fell asleep. When I awoke it was daylight. I jumped up and looked at Duncan. He was just stirring, and a moment later he opened his eyes.

"Where am I?" he asked, with a puzzled look at me.

"You're all right, Duncan," I replied. "Don't you remember?"

"Oh, yes, I do now. How my head hurts. Is there any water around?"

I went over to the faucet and drew him a glass. He sat up and gulped it down.

"Have we been here all night?"

"Yes."

"You saved me from those toughs that wanted to rob me last night?"

"Yes."

"I'm not dreaming?"

"No, you're not," I laughed. "I was just in the nick of time."

"I know it all. You saved me, brought me to this place, and put me to bed. Roger, you're a better fellow than I thought you were. You're a better fellow than I am."

"You ought to turn over a new leaf," I said.

"Don't preach, Roger."

"I'm not preaching. I'm only telling you something for your own good."

"I know it. I don't blame you. I've been doing wrong— sowing my wild oats. But they're all gone now. Just let me get straightened out and I'll be a different fellow, see if I'm not."

"I hope so with all my heart. What brought you to New York?"

He started.

"I—I came—I don't care to tell," he stammered.

"Were you going to Brooklyn?" I questioned, struck by a sudden idea.

"Why, how did you know?" he exclaimed.

"You have certain papers," I continued.

"Yes, I—" he felt in his pockets. "Why, where are they?"

"Are they in this?" I asked, suddenly remembering the notebook I had picked up, and producing it.

"Yes, yes, give them to me."

"I think I had better keep them," I replied decidedly.

# CHAPTER XXXIII

## IN BROOKLYN

I fully understood the value of the papers that were contained in the note-book. Mr. Aaron Woodward would not have persecuted me so closely had he not deemed them of great importance.

And when I told Duncan I would keep them, I meant what I said. It might not be right legally, but I was sure it was right morally, and that was enough to quiet my conscience.

"Better keep them?" repeated Duncan, as he sprang to his feet.

"Exactly."

"You have no right to do that."

"I don't know about that. I was arrested for having them, and what's the use of my having the name without the game?"

Duncan sank down on the edge of the bed again.

"If you had spoken to me like that yesterday, I'd have wanted to punch your head," he said. "But you're a good fellow,

Edward Stratemeyer

Roger, and I don't blame you for acting as you do. Do you know what the papers contain?"

"I think I do."

"They concern my father's affairs," he went on uneasily.

"And my father's as well," I added.

"Not so very much."

"I think so."

"Let me show you. Hand the papers over."

"Excuse me, Duncan, if I decline to do so. You, aided by Pultzer and others, stole them from your father's library, and then threw suspicion on me."

"I didn't throw suspicion on you. My father did that himself."

"You had nothing to do with that handkerchief?"

"I took the handkerchief by accident."

"Then I beg your pardon for having said so," I said heartily.

"Never mind, let that pass. I'll tell you what I'll do. Give me the papers and I will restore them to my father and tell him the truth."

"I must decline your offer."

"Why? Don't you believe I'll confess? If you don't I'll give you a written confession."

"No, it isn't that. I am going to keep the papers because they are valuable to me."

"What do you mean by valuable?" asked Duncan, his curiosity increasing.

"Just what I say."

"What will the old gent say when he hears of it?"

"I don't care what he says. He'll hear of a good deal more before long."

"How about the robbery at the Widow Canby's?"

"That will be straightened out, too."

There was a knock on the door, and, opening it, I was confronted by one of the servants.

"Mr. Strong here, sir?" he asked.

"That's my name."

"A gentleman below to see you, sir. Gave his name as Mr. Harrison."

"Tell him I will be down in a minute," I said.

"Now I'm ready to leave you," I went on to Duncan, when the servant had departed. "I advise you to take a good wash, get your breakfast, and take the first train home. Good-by."

"Yes, but, Roger—"

"By doing that you may be doing your father a greater

service than in any other way. You say you will turn over a new leaf, and I hope you will. If all goes as it should you will have a hard trial to stand before long. But do as I did when things went wrong in our family, bear up under it, and if you do what's right somebody is bound to respect you."

And, without waiting for a reply, I caught up my hat and hurried from the room.

I found Mr. Harrison waiting for me in the parlor.

"I thought I'd come over early," he explained. "I know young blood is impatient, and I half expected to find you gone."

"I didn't want to make a call before folks were up," I answered. "Besides, I have made quite an important discovery since we parted."

"Indeed."

"Yes. Come away from this place and I'll tell you. I don't want to meet Duncan Woodward again."

And as we walked away from the hotel I related the particulars about the note-book.

"You are gathering evidence by the wholesale," laughed Mr. Harrison. "You'll have more than enough to convict."

"I don't want to make a failure of it," I said firmly. "When I go to court I want a clear case from start to finish."

"Good! Strong, I admire your grit. Come in the restaurant, and while we have a bit of breakfast let us look over the papers. I declare, I was never before so interested in some one else's affairs."

And as we waited for our rolls, eggs, and coffee, we read the papers through carefully.

They gave much information, the most startling of which was that John Stumpy and Ferguson were one and the same person.

"That explains why Mr. Woodward made so many slips of the tongue when addressing him," I said.

"Here is another important thing," remarked Mr. Harrison; "a letter from this John Woodward stating that Mrs. Agatha Mitts knows of the forgeries. Now, if you can get this woman to testify against the two culprits, I think you will have a clear case."

"And that is just what I will force her to do," I said, with strong determination.

I could hardly wait to finish breakfast. Fortunately it did not take Mr. Harrison long to do so, and, five minutes later we were on our way to the ferry. The trip over the East River, near the big bridge, did not take long, and we soon stood on the opposite shore. Vannack Avenue was pretty well up town, and we took the elevated train to reach it.

"There is No. 648," said Mr. Harrison, pointing to a neat three-story brick building that stood in the middle of the block; "let us walk past first, and see if there is any name on the door."

We did so, and found a highly polished silver plate bearing the words:—

MRS. AGATHA MITTS
Boarding

"Perhaps it would be a good plan to find out something about the woman before we call on her," suggested my companion, after we had passed the house.

"There is a drug store on the corner," I said. "We can stop in there. No doubt they'll think we are looking for board."

"An excellent idea."

We walked down to the drug store. On entering, Mr. Harrison ordered a couple of glasses of soda water and then called the proprietor aside.

"Can you tell me anything about the lady that keeps the boarding-house below here?" he asked.

"Which one?"

"Mrs. Agatha Mitts."

"I've heard it's a very good house," was the noncommittal reply.

"You know the lady?"

"She comes in here once in a while for drugs."

"May I ask what kind of a woman she is?"

"Well, she's good enough in her way, though rather eccentric. I understand she furnishes good board, however. She has kept the house for many years."

"Has she many boarders?"

"Eight or ten. She used to have more. But they were rather a lively set and hurt the reputation of the place."

Mr. Harrison paid for the soda, and a second later we quitted the place.

"Not much information gained there," said my Chicago friend, when we were once again on the street.

"One thing is certain," I replied. "She is the right party. It would never have done to have tackled the wrong person."

"I guess the best thing for us to do is to call on the woman without waiting further."

"So I think."

"She may be a very hard person to manage. Strong, you must be careful of what you say."

"I shall, Mr. Harrison," I replied. "But that woman must do what is right or go to prison."

"I agree with you."

Ascending the steps of the house, I rang the bell. A tidy Irish girl answered the summons.

"Is Mrs. Agatha Mitts in?" I asked.

"Yes, sir."

"We would like to see her."

"Will you please step into the parlor?" went on the girl, and we did so.

"Who shall I say it is?"

"Mr. Harrison," put in my Western friend.

"Yes, sir."

The girl disappeared. My heart beat strongly. It seemed to me as if life and death hung upon the meeting that was to follow.

# CHAPTER XXXIV

## MRS. AGATHA. MITTS

I could not help but wonder, as I sat in the parlor with my friend Mr. Harrison, waiting for the appearance of Mrs. Agatha Mitts, what kind of a person the keeper of the boarding-house would prove to be.

For some reason the name suggested to me a tall, gaunt female with sharp features; and I was taken by surprise when a short, dumpy woman, with a round face, came wobbling in and asked what was wanted.

"This is Mrs. Agatha Mitts?" asked Mr. Harrison, as he arose.

"Yes, sir. And you are Mr. Harrison, I suppose. I don't remember you."

"I didn't think you would," laughed my friend from Chicago. "I am from the West, and have never before been in Brooklyn."

"Yes? Then your business with me is—? Perhaps you desire board?" and she smiled; first at him and then at me.

"No; we do not wish board," was the quiet reply. "We come to see you on business."

"And what is it?"

"We would like to see you privately."

"Certainly. Pray take a seat. I will close the doors."

She shut the folding doors leading to the sitting room, and then the door to the hall.

"Now I am quite at your service," she said, and peered at us rather sharply.

There was an awkward pause for a moment, and then Mr. Harrison went on bluntly:—

"Has Mr. Aaron Woodward or Chris Holtzmann been here since yesterday, madam?"

Mrs. Mitts started at the mention of the two names. Then she recovered herself.

"Whom did you say, sir?" she queried innocently.

Mr. Harrison repeated his question.

"Why, I really haven't heard of those two gentlemen in so long a time I've nearly forgotten them," she said sweetly.

"They weren't here yesterday?" I put in.

"No." And this time her tone was a trifle cold.

"Do you expect them to-day?" I went on.

"No, I don't." She paused a second. "Is that all you wish to know?"

"No, ma'am," I replied promptly. "There is a good deal more I wish to know."

"Who are you, if I may ask?"

"My name is Strong."

She looked puzzled for a moment.

"I don't recognize the name," she said, and then she suddenly turned pale.

"I am the son of Carson Strong, who was sent to prison for alleged forgery and the passing of worthless checks," I continued. "I suppose you remember the case."

"Har—hardly," she faltered. "I—I heard something of it, but not the particulars."

"That is strange, when you were so interested in it."

"I?" she repeated, in pretended surprise.

"Yes, madam," said Mr. Harrison. "You were very much interested."

"Who says so?"

"I say so," said I.

"You! You are only a boy."

"I suppose I am, but that doesn't make any difference. You

know all about the great wrong that has been done, and—"

"It is false! I know nothing!" she cried in anger.

"You know all, and we want you to tell as all you know before we leave this house."

Mrs. Agatha Mitts arose in a passion.

"I want you to get out of my house at once!" she ejaculated. "I won't stand your presence here another minute."

"Excuse me, madam; not so fast," said Mr. Harrison, calmly. "My young friend Strong is quite right in what he says."

"I don't care what you think about it," she snapped.

"Oh, yes, you do. Perhaps you don't know who I am," went on my Western friend, deliberately.

The sly insinuation had its effect. Evidently the woman had a swift vision of a detective in citizens' clothes before her mind's eye.

"You come in authority," she said faintly.

"We won't speak about that now," said Mr. Harrison. "All we want you to do is to make a complete confession of your knowledge of the affair."

"I haven't any knowledge."

"You have," I said. "You know everything. I have papers here belonging to Woodward, Holtzmann, and Ferguson to prove it. There is no use for you to deny it, and if you insist and make it necessary to call in the police—"

"No, no! Please don't do that, I beg of you," she cried.

"Then will you do as I wish?"

"But my reputation? It will be gone forever," she moaned.

"It will be gone anyway, if you have to go to prison," observed Mr. Harrison, sagely.

"And if I make a clean confession you will not prosecute me?" she asked eagerly.

"I'll promise you that," I said.

"You are not fooling me?"

"No, ma'am."

She sprang to her feet and paced the room several times.

"I'll do it," she cried. "They have never treated me right, and I do not care what becomes of them so long as I go clear. What do you wish me to do, gentlemen?"

I was nonplussed for an instant. Mr. Harrison helped me out.

"I will write out your confession and you can sign it," he said. "Have you ink and paper handy?"

"Yes."

Mrs. Mitts brought forth the material, and we all sat down again.

"Remember to give us only the plain facts," I said.

"I will," she returned sharply.

In a rather roundabout way she made her confession, if it could be called such. It filled several sheets of paper, and it took over half an hour. It contained but little more than what my readers already know or suspect. She knew positively that Mr. Aaron Woodward was the forger of the checks, Holtzmann had presented them, and Ferguson had so altered the daily reports that my father had unwittingly made a false showing on his books. About Weaver she knew nothing.

When once explained the whole matter was as clear as day.

When he had finished the writing, Mr. Harrison read the paper out loud, and after some hesitation the woman signed it, and then we both witnessed it.

"I guess our business here is at an end," said my Western friend.

"I think so," I replied. "But one thing more, Mrs. Mitts," I continued, turning to her. "If Mr. Woodward or Chris Holtzmann calls, I think you will find it advisable to keep this affair a secret."

"I will not be at home to them," she replied briefly.

"A good plan," said Mr. Harrison. "Now that you have done the right thing, the less you say about the matter the better for you."

A few minutes later, with the paper tucked safely in my pocket, we left the house. Mrs. Mitts watched us sharply from behind the half-closed blinds.

In half an hour we were down town and across the ferry

once more.

"I suppose you wish to get home as soon as possible," said Mr. Harrison, as we boarded a street-car to take us to his hotel.

"Yes, sir. My sister and the rest will be anxious to hear how I've made out, and besides I'm anxious to learn how things have gone since I have been away."

"I've no doubt of it."

"What do you intend to do?"

"I hardly know. I have some business, but I am quite interested in your case, and—"

"Would you like to go along! You'll be heartily welcome, sir."

"Thank you, I will. I want to see how this drama ends," said Mr. Harrison.

A little later I procured my valise, and we set out for Darbyville.

Edward Stratemeyer

# CHAPTER XXXV

## THE WIDOW CANBY'S MONEY

I am sure my readers will well understand why my thoughts were busy as the train rolled on its way to Newville. I could hardly realize that I held the proofs of my father's innocence in my possession; and I was strongly tempted several times to ask my kind Western friend to pinch me to make sure that I was really awake, and was not merely dreaming my good fortune.

Mr. Harrison probably guessed what was passing in my mind, for he placed a kindly hand upon my shoulder, and said, with a smile:—

"Does it seem almost too good to be true?"

"That's just it," I returned. "The events of the past week have so crowded on each other that I'm in a perfect whirl."

"You will have a little more excitement before it is over."

"I suppose so. But now that I know it is all right I shall not mind it. I wonder if I couldn't send my father the good news by telegraph?"

"You can easily enough. But don't you think you had better wait until all is settled? You might raise false hopes."

"No fear; Aaron Woodward is guilty beyond a doubt. But I will wait if you think best."

It was not long before the train rolled into Newville. On alighting Mr. Harrison insisted on hiring a cab, and in this we bowled swiftly on our way to Darbyville. As we passed out of the city and up on the country road I wondered how matters had progressed during my absence. Had the merchant returned home?

At Darbyville a crowd of men gazed at us with curious eyes. Among them was Parsons the constable and others who knew me.

"Hello, you back again?" shouted Parsons.

"Yes, indeed," I replied. "I suppose you didn't expect me so soon?"

"I'll allow as how I didn't expect you at all," he returned, with a grin.

"Well, you were mistaken. I'm back, and back to stay," said I.

My heart beat high as we turned into the side road that led to the Widow Canby's house. I strained my eyes to catch sight of the first one who might appear. It was my Uncle Enos. He was doing a bit of mending on the front fence. As soon as he saw me he threw down his hammer, and ran toward us.

"Well, well, Roger, struck port again, have you? Glad you're back."

And he shook my right hand hard.

"My friend, Mr. Harrison, from Chicago," said I. "This is my uncle, Captain Enos Moss."

They had hardly finished hand-shaking, when Kate and the Widow Canby came out of the house.

"Oh, Roger, I'm so glad you're back!" cried Kate. And then she looked earnestly into my eyes. "Did you—did, you—"

"Yes, Kate, I've succeeded. Father's innocence can be proven."

"Oh, thank God!" cried my sister, and the tears of joy started from her eyes. I felt like crying, too, and soon, somehow, there was hardly a dry eye in the group.

"You must have had a hard time of it," sail the Widow Canby.

"My kind friend here helped me a good deal," I said.

Mr. Harrison was introduced to the others, and soon we were seated, on the piazza, and I was relating my experiences.

The interest of my listeners grew as I went on. They could hardly believe it possible that Mr. Aaron Woodward, with all his outward show of gentlemanliness, was such a thoroughly bad man. When I came to speak of John Stumpy, alias Ferguson, Kate burst out:—

"I declare, I've almost forgotten. I've got good news, too. This very morning I went hunting again and picked up the paper that was lost. I was trying to read it when you drove up. Here it is."

And my sister handed over Nicholas Weaver's dying statement.

"It is hardly of use now," I said. "Still, it will make the evidence against Mr. Woodward so much stronger."

"I've discovered that this Nick Weaver was a chum of Woodward's," said Uncle Enos.

"A chum?"

"Yes. He came from Chicago."

"From Chicago!" I ejaculated.

"Exactly."

Meanwhile Mr. Harrison was examining the statement, which Kate had produced from her dress pocket.

"I see it all," he cried. "Nicholas Weaver was the man who helped Holtzmann concoct the scheme whereby a relative in Chicago was supposed to have died and willed Aaron Woodward all his money."

"I see. But why did he leave the statement?" I asked.

"Because, he says here, Woodward did not treat him right. This Ferguson or Stumpy was a friend to Weaver, and the paper was gotten up to bring Woodward to terms."

That explanation was clear enough, and I could easily understand why John Stumpy had come to Darbyville, and how it was the merchant had treated him with so much consideration.

"And there is another thing to tell you, Roger," put in the Widow Canby. "Something I know you will be greatly pleased to hear."

"What is it?" I asked, in considerable curiosity.

"I have evidence to show that this John Stumpy was the man who robbed me of my money. Of course I knew it was so when Kate and you said so, but outsiders now know it."

"And how?"

"Miles Nanson saw the man running from the house. He was hurrying to get a doctor for his wife, who was very sick, and he didn't stop to question the fellow."

"But why didn't he speak of it before?" I asked. "He might have saved us a deal of trouble."

"He never heard of the robbery until last night, his wife has been so sick. He can testify to seeing the man."

"I'm glad of that," I said. "But unfortunately, that doesn't restore the money."

"No, I suppose not. This Stumpy still has it."

"No; he claims to have lost it," I returned, and I related the particulars as I had overheard them in the boarding-house on the opposite side of the Pass River.

"I wish I could find it—the money, I mean—as I did the papers," put in Kate.

"Where did he jump over the fence?" I asked suddenly.

"Down by the crab-apple tree," said Uncle Enos.

"Have you looked there?" queried Mr. Harrison.

"No," said Kate; "you don't think—" she began.

"There is nothing like looking," said my Western friend, slowly.

"I guess you're right," I replied, "and the sooner the better."

In a minute I was out of the house. Kate was close on my heels, and together we made our way to the orchard, followed by the others.

"Now, let me see," I went on. "If he went over the fence here he must have vaulted over. I'll try that, and note how the money might have dropped."

I placed my hands on the top rail and sprang up to vault over. As my head bent over, my eyes caught sight of an object lying in the hole of the fence post.

I picked it up. It was the Widow Canby's pocketbook.

Edward Stratemeyer

# CHAPTER XXXVI

## "ALL'S WELL THAT ENDS WELL"

Of course I was highly delighted with the success of my search, and as I brought forth the pocketbook all the others gave a cry of surprise.

"You've got it, Roger!" ejaculated my uncle. "You've got it, just as sure as guns is guns!"

"So I have," I replied, as coolly as I could, though I was at the top notch of excitement.

"Better examine it," put in Mr. Harrison, cautiously. "It may be empty."

"Empty!" cried Kate in dismay, and the word sent a chill through my own heart.

With nervous fingers I tore the pocketbook open. I suppose I ought to have given it to the widow, but I was too excited to think of what was just right and what was not.

"The money was in a piece of newspaper," said the Widow Canby. "I had—ah, there it is!"

And sure enough, there it was—nearly three hundred dollars—safe and sound.

I almost felt like dancing a jig, and could not refrain from throwing up my hat, which I did in such a way that it caught in a limb of a tree, and forced me to climb up to recover it.

As I was about jumping to the ground I heard a buggy pass on the road. Looking down, I was surprised to see that it contained Mr. Aaron Woodward and Chris Holtzmann. On seeing the party on the ground below, the merchant stopped his horse and jumped out.

"How do you do, Mrs. Canby?" he said, as he came over to the fence without catching sight of me.

"Pretty well, Mr. Woodward," was the widow's reply.

"Have you heard anything of your money yet?" went on the merchant, with apparent concern.

"Oh, yes—" and the widow hesitated.

My sister whispered something in her ear.

"It was just found," said Kate.

The merchant gave a start.

"You don't mean it!" he cried. "Where?"

"Down here by the fence."

"Who put it there?" asked Mr. Woodward, sharply.

"No one. It was dropped by John Stumpy."

"Humph! Perhaps so!" sneered the merchant.

"It's true," exclaimed Kate, stoutly.

"More likely by your brother Roger."

"Avast there!" cried Uncle Enos. "You're saying too much."

"I don't think so," replied Mr. Woodward, in deep sarcasm. "Of course you want to shield the boy all you can, but I 'm sure in my mind that he is guilty."

"And I'm positive in my own mind that I'm innocent," said I, and I jumped to the ground.

"Roger Strong!" he cried, stepping back in surprise; and I saw Chris Holtzmann give a start. "Where did you come from?"

"I came from—up a tree," I returned lightly, and I may add that never before had I felt in such particularly good humor.

"Don't trifle with me," he cried in anger. "Answer my question."

"I will when I get ready."

"You refuse?"

"Oh, no. But I'm not compelled to answer, understand that, Mr. Aaron Woodward. I'll answer because I choose to do so."

"Never mind," he snapped. "Where have you been?"

"To Chicago—as you know—and to Brooklyn."

"To Brooklyn!" he cried, growing pale.

"Yes, sir, to see Mrs. Agatha Mitts."

"And did you see her?" he faltered.

"Yes, sir."

"And she—" he began.

"What she said or did will be produced in court later on," put in Mr. Harrison.

"Eh?" the merchant wheeled around. "Who are you?"

"My name is James Harrison. I am from Chicago. I am this boy's friend, and I am here to see justice done."

"What do you mean?"

"I mean that you and your colleagues—Chris Holtzmann there, John Stumpy, alias Ferguson, and the late Nicholas Weaver—have foully wronged this boy's father."

"It's a lie!" cried Aaron Woodward, with a quivering lip.

"It's the truth," I said. "The plain truth, and I can prove every word of it."

"Prove it!"

"Yes, in every detail, Mr. Aaron Woodward. I have worked hard fighting for honor, but I have won. Soon my father shall be free, and for aught I know to the contrary, you will occupy his place in prison."

"I!" cried the merchant, in horror. "A likely thing!"

"We shall see," I said. "In the meantime be careful of what you say against me, or I will have you arrested before sundown."

Mr. Woodward gave me a look that was savageness itself. Apparently he was on the verge of giving way to a burst of temper. But he seemed to think better of it, and turning, he jumped into his buggy and drove away.

It was the last time I ever saw him. On the following day Mr. Harrison, Uncle Enos, and myself drove down to Newville and engaged a first-class lawyer to take up the case. This legal gentleman pushed matters so fast that on the following Monday all the papers necessary for Woodward's arrest were ready for execution.

The officers came to Darbyville late in the afternoon to secure their man. They were told that Mr. Woodward had gone to New York on business. They waited for him the remainder of the day and all of the next.

It was useless. The highly respected head merchant of Darbyville did not appear; and an examination showed that he had mortgaged his house and his business, and taken every cent of cash with him.

It was an open acknowledgment of his guilt, and Kate was for letting it go at that.

"It will do no good to have him locked up," she said.

"One thing is certain, sech a rascal ain't fit to be at liberty," put in my Uncle Enos.

"He may turn around and rob somebody else," added the Widow Canby.

"That's just it," I said; and determined to bring the man to justice, I set a detective on his track.

The search was successful, for in a week Aaron Woodward was caught in Boston, preparing to embark for Europe. He was brought back to Newville to await the action of the grand jury. But he never came to trial. In less than a week he was found in his cell one morning, dying. Rather than face the humiliation of going to jail he had taken his life. What became of Duncan I did not know for a long while until, through Mr. Harrison, I learned that he was in Chicago working for one of the railroads. He had the making of a good fellow in him, and I trust that he became one. Chris Holtzmann disappeared, and his Palace of Pleasure is a thing of the past. John Stumpy went to Texas, and I heard that Pultzer went with him.

It was not long before my father received his pardon and came home. I cannot express the joy that all of us experienced when he came forth from prison, not only a free man, but also bearing the proofs of his innocence. We were all there to greet him, and as my sister Kate rushed into his arms I felt that fighting for honor meant a good deal.

Five years have gone by. My father and I are now in business in Newville. We live in Darbyville, along with my uncle,—who married the Widow Canby,—and my sister Kate.

Holland & Mack have recovered all that was stolen from them. They were profuse in their apologies to my father, and offered him a good situation, which he declined.

We are all happy—especially Kate and I. During off hours

we are all but inseparable. I like my work, and expect some day to be a leading merchant. The clouds that hung over the family honor have passed, and sunshine seems to have come to stay, and that being so I will bid my readers good-by.

THE END

# ABOUT THE AUTHOR

**Edward Stratemeyer** (October 4, 1862 - May 10, 1930). Born in Elizabeth, New Jersey he was an American publisher and writer of books for children. He created the Hardy Boys, Bobbsey Twins, Nancy Drew, Rover Boys, and Tom Swift series, among others.

Strameyer used a number of pen names, including Arthur M. Winfield. He wrote his first book and submitted to a publisher under this name which he is said to have chosen partly as a joke because it is a play on words, with "Arthur" being close to "author" and "Winfield" indicating his willingness to "win" and become famous as a children's book author.

Stratemeyer pioneered the technique of producing long-running, consistent series of books using a team of freelance authors to write standardized novels, which were published under a pen name owned by his company. Through his Stratemeyer Syndicate Stratemeyer produced short plot summaries for the novels in each series, which he sent to other writers who completed the story, writing a specified number of pages and chapters. Each book would begin with an introduction of the characters and would be interrupted at the first cliffhanger for a quick recap of all the previous books in the series.

# Choose from Thousands of 1stWorldLibrary Classics By

A. M. Barnard
Ada Leverson
Adolphus William Ward
Aesop
Agatha Christie
Alexander Aaronsohn
Alexander Kielland
Alexandre Dumas
Alfred Gatty
Alfred Ollivant
Alice Duer Miller
Alice Turner Curtis
Alice Dunbar
Allen Chapman
Alleyne Ireland
Ambrose Bierce
Amelia E. Barr
Amory H. Bradford
Andrew Lang
Andrew McFarland Davis
Andy Adams
Angela Brazil
Anna Alice Chapin
Anna Sewell
Annie Besant
Annie Hamilton Donnell
Annie Payson Call
Annie Roe Carr
Annonaymous
Anton Chekhov
Archibald Lee Fletcher
Arnold Bennett
Arthur C. Benson
Arthur Conan Doyle
Arthur M. Winfield
Arthur Ransome
Arthur Schnitzler
Arthur Train
Atticus
B.H. Baden-Powell
B. M. Bower
B. C. Chatterjee
Baroness Emmuska Orczy
Baroness Orczy
Basil King
Bayard Taylor
Ben Macomber
Bertha Muzzy Bower
Bjornstjerne Bjornson

Booth Tarkington
Boyd Cable
Bram Stoker
C. Collodi
C. E. Orr
C. M. Ingleby
Carolyn Wells
Catherine Parr Traill
Charles A. Eastman
Charles Amory Beach
Charles Dickens
Charles Dudley Warner
Charles Farrar Browne
Charles Ives
Charles Kingsley
Charles Klein
Charles Hanson Towne
Charles Lathrop Pack
Charles Romyn Dake
Charles Whibley
Charles Willing Beale
Charlotte M. Braeme
Charlotte M. Yonge
Charlotte Perkins Stetson
Clair W. Hayes
Clarence Day Jr.
Clarence E. Mulford
Clemence Housman
Confucius
Coningsby Dawson
Cornelis DeWitt Wilcox
Cyril Burleigh
D. H. Lawrence
Daniel Defoe
David Garnett
Dinah Craik
Don Carlos Janes
Donald Keyhoe
Dorothy Kilner
Dougan Clark
Douglas Fairbanks
E. Nesbit
E. P. Roe
E. Phillips Oppenheim
E. S. Brooks
Earl Barnes
Edgar Rice Burroughs
Edith Van Dyne
Edith Wharton

Edward Everett Hale
Edward J. O'Biren
Edward S. Ellis
Edwin L. Arnold
Eleanor Atkins
Eleanor Hallowell Abbott
Eliot Gregory
Elizabeth Gaskell
Elizabeth McCracken
Elizabeth Von Arnim
Ellem Key
Emerson Hough
Emilie F. Carlen
Emily Bronte
Emily Dickinson
Enid Bagnold
Enilor Macartney Lane
Erasmus W. Jones
Ernie Howard Pie
Ethel May Dell
Ethel Turner
Ethel Watts Mumford
Eugene Sue
Eugenie Foa
Eugene Wood
Eustace Hale Ball
Evelyn Everett-green
Everard Cotes
F. H. Cheley
F. J. Cross
F. Marion Crawford
Fannie E. Newberry
Federick Austin Ogg
Ferdinand Ossendowski
Fergus Hume
Florence A. Kilpatrick
Fremont B. Deering
Francis Bacon
Francis Darwin
Frances Hodgson Burnett
Frances Parkinson Keyes
Frank Gee Patchin
Frank Harris
Frank Jewett Mather
Frank L. Packard
Frank V. Webster
Frederic Stewart Isham
Frederick Trevor Hill
Frederick Winslow Taylor

Friedrich Kerst
Friedrich Nietzsche
Fyodor Dostoyevsky
G.A. Henty
G.K. Chesterton
Gabrielle E. Jackson
Garrett P. Serviss
Gaston Leroux
George A. Warren
George Ade
Geroge Bernard Shaw
George Cary Eggleston
George Durston
George Ebers
George Eliot
George Gissing
George MacDonald
George Meredith
George Orwell
George Sylvester Viereck
George Tucker
George W. Cable
George Wharton James
Gertrude Atherton
Gordon Casserly
Grace E. King
Grace Gallatin
Grace Greenwood
Grant Allen
Guillermo A. Sherwell
Gulielma Zollinger
Gustav Flaubert
H. A. Cody
H. B. Irving
H.C. Bailey
H. G. Wells
H. H. Munro
H. Irving Hancock
H. R. Naylor
H. Rider Haggard
H. W. C. Davis
Haldeman Julius
Hall Caine
Hamilton Wright Mabie
Hans Christian Andersen
Harold Avery
Harold McGrath
Harriet Beecher Stowe
Harry Castlemon
Harry Coghill
Harry Houidini

Hayden Carruth
Helent Hunt Jackson
Helen Nicolay
Hendrik Conscience
Hendy David Thoreau
Henri Barbusse
Henrik Ibsen
Henry Adams
Henry Ford
Henry Frost
Henry James
Henry Jones Ford
Henry Seton Merriman
Henry W Longfellow
Herbert A. Giles
Herbert Carter
Herbert N. Casson
Herman Hesse
Hildegard G. Frey
Homer
Honore De Balzac
Horace B. Day
Horace Walpole
Horatio Alger Jr.
Howard Pyle
Howard R. Garis
Hugh Lofting
Hugh Walpole
Humphry Ward
Ian Maclaren
Inez Haynes Gillmore
Irving Bacheller
Isabel Cecilia Williams
Isabel Hornibrook
Israel Abrahams
Ivan Turgenev
J.G.Austin
J. Henri Fabre
J. M. Barrie
J. M. Walsh
J. Macdonald Oxley
J. R. Miller
J. S. Fletcher
J. S. Knowles
J. Storer Clouston
J. W. Duffield
Jack London
Jacob Abbott
James Allen
James Andrews
James Baldwin

James Branch Cabell
James DeMille
James Joyce
James Lane Allen
James Lane Allen
James Oliver Curwood
James Oppenheim
James Otis
James R. Driscoll
Jane Abbott
Jane Austen
Jane L. Stewart
Janet Aldridge
Jens Peter Jacobsen
Jerome K. Jerome
Jessie Graham Flower
John Buchan
John Burroughs
John Cournos
John F. Kennedy
John Gay
John Glasworthy
John Habberton
John Joy Bell
John Kendrick Bangs
John Milton
John Philip Sousa
John Taintor Foote
Jonas Lauritz Idemil Lie
Jonathan Swift
Joseph A. Altsheler
Joseph Carey
Joseph Conrad
Joseph E. Badger Jr
Joseph Hergesheimer
Joseph Jacobs
Jules Vernes
Julian Hawthrone
Julie A Lippmann
Justin Huntly McCarthy
Kakuzo Okakura
Karle Wilson Baker
Kate Chopin
Kenneth Grahame
Kenneth McGaffey
Kate Langley Bosher
Kate Langley Bosher
Katherine Cecil Thurston
Katherine Stokes
L. A. Abbot
L. T. Meade

L. Frank Baum
Latta Griswold
Laura Dent Crane
Laura Lee Hope
Laurence Housman
Lawrence Beasley
Leo Tolstoy
Leonid Andreyev
Lewis Carroll
Lewis Sperry Chafer
Lilian Bell
Lloyd Osbourne
Louis Hughes
Louis Joseph Vance
Louis Tracy
Louisa May Alcott
Lucy Fitch Perkins
Lucy Maud Montgomery
Luther Benson
Lydia Miller Middleton
Lyndon Orr
M. Corvus
M. H. Adams
Margaret E. Sangster
Margret Howth
Margaret Vandercook
Margaret W. Hungerford
Margret Penrose
Maria Edgeworth
Maria Thompson Daviess
Mariano Azuela
Marion Polk Angellotti
Mark Overton
Mark Twain
Mary Austin
Mary Catherine Crowley
Mary Cole
Mary Hastings Bradley
Mary Roberts Rinehart
Mary Rowlandson
M. Wollstonecraft Shelley
Maud Lindsay
Max Beerbohm
Myra Kelly
Nathaniel Hawthrone
Nicolo Machiavelli
O. F. Walton
Oscar Wilde

Owen Johnson
P.G. Wodehouse
Paul and Mabel Thorne
Paul G. Tomlinson
Paul Severing
Percy Brebner
Percy Keese Fitzhugh
Peter B. Kyne
Plato
Quincy Allen
R. Derby Holmes
R. L. Stevenson
R. S. Ball
Rabindranath Tagore
Rahul Alvares
Ralph Bonehill
Ralph Henry Barbour
Ralph Victor
Ralph Waldo Emmerson
Rene Descartes
Ray Cummings
Rex Beach
Rex E. Beach
Richard Harding Davis
Richard Jefferies
Richard Le Gallienne
Robert Barr
Robert Frost
Robert Gordon Anderson
Robert L. Drake
Robert Lansing
Robert Lynd
Robert Michael Ballantyne
Robert W. Chambers
Rosa Nouchette Carey
Rudyard Kipling
Saint Augustine
Samuel B. Allison
Samuel Hopkins Adams
Sarah Bernhardt
Sarah C. Hallowell
Selma Lagerlof
Sherwood Anderson
Sigmund Freud
Standish O'Grady
Stanley Weyman
Stella Benson
Stella M. Francis

Stephen Crane
Stewart Edward White
Stijn Streuvels
Swami Abhedananda
Swami Parmananda
T. S. Ackland
T. S. Arthur
The Princess Der Ling
Thomas A. Janvier
Thomas A Kempis
Thomas Anderton
Thomas Bailey Aldrich
Thomas Bulfinch
Thomas De Quincey
Thomas Dixon
Thomas H. Huxley
Thomas Hardy
Thomas More
Thornton W. Burgess
U. S. Grant
Upton Sinclair
Valentine Williams
Various Authors
Vaughan Kester
Victor Appleton
Victor G. Durham
Victoria Cross
Virginia Woolf
Wadsworth Camp
Walter Camp
Walter Scott
Washington Irving
Wilbur Lawton
Wilkie Collins
Willa Cather
Willard F. Baker
William Dean Howells
William le Queux
W. Makepeace Thackeray
William W. Walter
William Shakespeare
Winston Churchill
Yei Theodora Ozaki
Yogi Ramacharaka
Young E. Allison
Zane Grey